Tales of the Were

Slade

BIANCA D'ARC

First electronic publication: March 2013
First print publication: April 2013

ISBN: 1483967581
ISBN-13: 978-1483967585

DEDICATION

As always, my work is dedicated to my family, who allow me the freedom to do what I love and the encouragement to keep trying, even when I get discouraged. You're the best!

I also want to acknowledge Valerie Tibbs of Tibbs Design for working with me on the cover for this book. It was worth the effort, because I think it's really gorgeous. Thank you, V!

Special thanks to Virginia Ettel for her help in sorting out the many Redstones and their friends. And many thanks to Peg McChesney for helping sort out the voice recognition mess. Eek!

I'd also like to give a shout out to the Wild West Wednesday crew and the Book Obsessed Chicks, who have made the past year or so a lot of fun!

And Mom, if you're watching, you know how much I miss and love you. Thanks for encouraging me to follow my dream. Everything I have achieved over the past seven years is thanks to you.

PRAISE FOR BIANCA D'ARC

"This is the Bianca D'Arc I've been waiting for! ...romance that's hotter than hot and sweeter than sweet." – Reviews by Molly on *Tales of the Were:* **Rocky**

"A truly fantastic read! With a page-turning plot, dynamic characters and plenty of heat, readers will devour every last delicious page." - RT Book Reviews Magazine TOP PICK! 4.5 Stars for *Brotherhood of Blood:* **Wolf Hills**

"...Fantasy romance readers will lap up this one (and the rest of the series)." — Marlene Harris, Seattle P.L. on **The Dragon Healer** for Library Journal

OTHER TITLES BY BIANCA D'ARC

AUTHOR'S NOTE

The internal chronology of my paranormal stories probably needs a little explaining. In a perfect world, all these books would have come out in the order in which the events in the books happen. Unfortunately, due to publisher issues all along the way, they have come out in a slightly different order.

The events in my earlier-published book, *Sweeter Than Wine*, actually happen after the events in both *Rocky* and this book, *Slade*.

PROLOGUE

Nevada

The Priestess raised her arms to the morning sun and gave thanks to the Lady she served for the good friends she'd found in this new shifter community. Kate had been on her own too long. It was good to find welcome among the odd collection of shifters of all species. They were quickly becoming close friends, even if she lacked the fur to run with them when the moon was full—or any other time they wanted to prowl the desert.

The day had dawned clear, the desert wind softly blowing tiny bits of sand around her feet as she performed her ritual, calling on the magic that was hers by gift of the Goddess she served. It was a cleansing ritual, meant to purify the land surrounding the small house she'd been given to live in by the Alpha. Griffon was a good Alpha, watching out for all his people—the cougars of his immediate Clan, as well as the large numbers of shifters that worked for him. He treated them all like family and made sure they had nice homes and good pay for the work they did.

Kate felt the energies rising at her call. The rhythm of the desert was new to her, but she liked it. Life was so much closer to the edge of survival here in the unforgiving wild lands, even if they were slowly being tamed by the human sprawl only a few miles away.

Regular people couldn't really feel the magic all around them, and she could only guess at what the shifters could sense. What she wouldn't give to know what they knew.

But that was not her path. She served the Light and helped the Lady's followers wherever she could. That was her mission and her duty in the life she had forged for herself. It had been a long, strange path that had led her here, but she liked the life she was creating among the cougars and wolves, bears and raptors who had gathered around Griffon Redstone.

She felt the energy rise and welcome her to the neighborhood, as it were. The energy of the land and the shifters who lived there. The power of Mother Earth. Welcoming. Sacred. Alarmed?

Something shifted in the energy of the Earth. A sudden change from good to...evil? There was no evil inherent in the area. Kate had checked. Visiting evil then. Someone — or some*thing* — intent on doing something bad. Serving the dark. Not the Light.

She needed to...

A sudden crescendo of power caught her unaware. Kate doubled over in pain as her magical senses took a blow she was totally unprepared for. A pulse of evil power so intense, it almost blacked her out.

She'd let down her shields to touch the heart of Mother Earth and been caught off guard. She'd been foolish to think that nothing could harm her—or anyone—in a development full of shifters.

Something bad was out there. Something that had just killed.

Oh, dear Goddess.

Montana

"There's been some trouble at the Redstone homestead," Rafe announced as soon as Slade walked into the office the Lords shared. Rafe and his twin brother, Tim, were standing behind their desks, clearly agitated.

"What kind of trouble?" Slade asked, stopping to shut the door behind him. From the looks on their faces, he could already tell the news was not going to be good.

"Bad trouble," Tim growled.

"Someone killed the matriarch of the Redstone Clan." Rafe paused, his eyes narrowing to steely slits. "She was skinned."

Slade said nothing but the growl that rose in his chest could not be denied. He was both sickened and angered at the thought of what had happened to that poor woman. It was desecration. Defilement at the most basic level.

The Redstone Clan was one of the most prominent bands of cougar shifters in North America. They also ran a huge construction company with nationwide reach that employed many, many shifters of all kinds. They treated their people well and had the highest standards of both services and protections for their employees. The shifters who worked for them were free to be themselves—to use their preternatural strength and skill without fear of betraying exactly what they were to the human world.

Redstone Construction was a place where shifters could be shifters. They could use their skills without fear of discovery, and were paid well—and treated well—for it. The Redstones were beloved in the community and it was abhorrent to think someone would treat the family—especially the dearly loved matriarch—in such a way.

Skinning a shifter was the highest insult. The most disgusting desecration. It was evil. Pure and simple.

"You want me to hunt the killer?" Slade asked, unable to control the gruffness of his voice. His inner cat wanted to rend and tear. To kill those who would treat a female so brutally.

"Yes," Tim answered.

"As you can imagine, the Alpha is beside himself," Rafe explained further. "He's just lost his mother and the entire extended Clan depends on him. Redstone Construction covers more than just cats. It's cross-species and far-reaching. Which may be why they were targeted. The Alpha is hunting already, but it's clear from our telephone conversation with him that he's not stable."

"He's out there with his brothers and not one of them is thinking clearly," Tim added.

"They believe the killer is hiding in the city. Their current base is outside Las Vegas. The cougars' tracking skills are good, but not that good. They're more used to wilderness, not pavement. We need you to keep a lid on the situation. You're a cat and for some reason nobody has seen fit to explain to us, the other felines respect you more than anyone else. Hell, it's like they revere you or something." Rafe ran a frustrated hand through his hair. "One day, you'll have to explain that to us, but for now I think you're the only one they'll listen to."

Tim picked up the thread of his twin's words. "Go to them. Help them find the killer. Get justice for the matriarch. But most important of all, keep our secret. Don't let those cougars get so out of control in their grief that they betray us all to the humans. You're on the hunt, but you're also on damage control. Those boys are just unstable enough to not care who sees them shapeshift or use their other natural abilities. They're dangerous to us, to themselves, and to every single shifter who works for them right now."

"If humans realize Redstone Construction is run by a Clan of cougar shifters, we have no doubt that everyone who works for them will come under suspicion," Rafe added. "That puts a hell of a lot of our people at risk."

"We'll be stretched thin without you to oversee security here and the new bear cubs are of the highest importance. I hope you understand that we can't spare any of your team. They know our setup best, and this could all be some kind of feint. But we're sending for other resources," Tim said with a bite in his voice. "The Spec Ops group in Wyoming is on call for you. And some of those seals in the Northeast have pledged to come running, if needed. That's your call, Slade. Do your thing. Track the killer, or killers. Assess the situation."

"And if you need reinforcements, our best warriors are at your disposal," Rafe completed his twin's thoughts. "Call them. They can be there in a matter of hours. And if you think it's wise, feel free to pre-position them just in case. We're covering the costs. This could be too important to leave to chance."

Slade realized at that moment just how explosive his mission might be. The fate of not just the Redstone Clan, but of hundreds—possibly thousands—of shifters of all kinds was riding on his shoulders.

He knew he was up to the challenge. Slade hadn't met an obstacle yet that he couldn't climb over, barrel through or go around. A couple of grief-stricken cougars was something he could handle. Especially with the cavalry at his beck and call. He knew most of the shifter Special Operators Tim and Rafe had put on alert. Slade had worked with a lot of them over the years and knew they were the best of the best.

Would he need that kind of backup? Slade wasn't sure yet. But it was good to know he could call upon his brothers-in-arms should the need arise.

Subtlety was Slade's stock and trade, though. He usually preferred to handle his missions alone. He was a cat, after all, and liked to prowl solo. He enjoyed the hunt, the chase, and ultimately, the kill. Slade would take great pleasure in disemboweling the humans who had caused such grief among shifters and put so many lives on the line.

Justice would be served and Slade was just the cat to serve it up. Sliced. Diced. And very, very cold.

CHAPTER ONE

Slade went through the background information he had on the Redstone Clan one last time as the plane approached Las Vegas. Glancing out the window he could see the pyramid shaped hotel that always made him shake his head when he landed here. Next to it was a castle and nearby was a replica of some of the biggest tourist attractions in New York. Down the street was a short Eiffel Tower and inside yet another casino on the famous strip, was a much cleaner and less aromatic replica of the canals of Venice.

One thing was certain. It was a crazy town.

That was probably one of the reasons the Redstones had recently moved the base of their very successful construction business out to this modern oasis in the middle of the desert. Very little could shock the jaded denizens of Las Vegas, so the increased concentration of shifters was probably a lot less noticeable in this city than it would have been in many other western metropolises.

Redstone Construction had been, and still was, the primary contractor on many new housing developments. They had built a reputation on the fact that they put their own unique stamp on the distinctive homes and communities they created.

More recently, they'd become a key player in the construction of casinos and high rises that had been going up all over Las Vegas. Raptors were natural iron workers. They had no fear of heights. As a result, many werehawks had long been manning the night shift as iron workers. If they somehow fell, nobody would see them shift and fly away in the dark. But on a Redstone Construction site, they could work day shift and nobody would be the wiser because every other man on site was a shifter too.

As the plane landed, Slade closed his files and got ready to deplane with the rest of the passengers. Not one raised any of his senses. The flight crew and passengers were no more than simple humans, going about their ordinary lives. They had no idea of the shit storm going down in the supernatural community and the escalating war between good and evil of the foulest kind.

He got off the plane and headed through the terminal. The one-armed bandits in the airport always made him chuckle. Las Vegas was indeed a strange place when compared to the rest of the country. He made his way to the car rental counter and picked up the keys for an SUV he'd arranged for ahead of time. Slade didn't know where this mission would take him. It was best to have a utility vehicle that would work as well in the desert as it did in the city.

Thankfully, Slade didn't have to use one of the many garish hotels for his stay in Sin City. Once the Lords had informed the Redstones they were sending help, the cougars had offered their hospitality. Slade drove to the outskirts of the city, to one of the outlying residential developments. This one was in an upscale section and the homes were large, with big backyards.

The moment he entered the gated community, Slade knew this was a place populated almost exclusively by shifters. He could feel the animal magic in the air and his sensitive nose picked up many different species of *were*. Lots of felines of course, plus a couple of different concentrations of canine species and more than a few hints of raptor.

Slade arrived at the house he'd been instructed to seek. It was large, but not opulent in an unseemly way. It was big enough to house an extended family of cat shifters and still give them all room to roam. Wolves liked to live in close Packs, but cats were more independent of each other and needed room to stretch. It made sense to Slade that the Alpha of the Cougar Clan and his family would want a place like this.

But something was very off in this community right now. There was a pervasive feeling of worry, sadness and an almost uncontrollable anger. Fury. Shock. Disgust. Killing rage.

Not good.

Slade parked his rented SUV at the curb out front. It was a silent message. He wanted everyone to know he was there and that he approached openly, posing no threat. Slade moved quickly up the front walk to the door. He pushed the doorbell button and waited while someone inside walked tiredly up to answer. He could hear the fatigue in the way the woman's feet dragged against the thick carpet on the other side of the door.

She opened it and they both just stood there for a moment, taking stock of each other. Slade read speculation in her eyes as she looked him over, but it wasn't the male-female sort of perusal. No, this was on another level entirely. A magical level. Her power sparked off his on the ethereal plane where magic lived. "Well now," she drawled, continuing to size him up. "You're something unexpected. You're not a cougar, are you." It was phrased as a question, but the tone implied she knew darn well he wasn't any sort of regular cat.

"I'm Slade. The Lords sent me to help track." He thought it best to keep his explanations simple until he learned why a witch was answering the door in what he'd assumed was a purely cougar household.

She smiled, her expression open and welcoming. "They said you were on your way. I'm Valerie Faber-Redstone. I'm married into the Clan. My husband is..." She looked over her shoulder, and her stance changed. Slade sensed the approach of her mate and he wasn't surprised to see a large, blond-headed man step up behind her a moment later. "Well," she said, turning back to Slade. "This is my husband, Keith Redstone."

Keith slid one clearly possessive arm around his wife's middle, tugging her back against him. They looked right together and Slade knew this was a true mating. He could see the magic around them both swirling and twining together, making both stronger together than either one was alone. Interesting.

"Slade," he repeated his name, as he took off his sunglasses, waiting to see what the male cougar would make of him.

"Jeepers creepers, get a load of them peepers," Valerie said in a low, amused tone. "You're not like the other cats, are you?"

Slade knew the witch saw the difference in his eyes. To most people they just looked intensely blue, but to those with magesight, sometimes...they glowed.

"I'll be damned," Keith whistled between his teeth. "If you can't calm things down, I don't know who can. Thanks for coming." The couple rearranged themselves, Valerie moving out of the doorway so Keith could offer Slade his hand in welcome.

They shook hands and Slade got the feel of the cougar's surprising magic. Even more surprising was the shield he walked through as he entered the house. More magic. A spell of protection had been put on the portal. Slade's eyebrow rose as he looked significantly at Valerie.

"I put protective spells on the house as soon as we arrived," she answered his unspoken question.

"They're very potent," Slade commented, revealing a bit of his own arcane knowledge to see what they'd make of him. It was clear these two already recognized that he wasn't entirely *were*. Or at least, not any kind of *were* they'd ever met before.

Slade was used to being the odd cat out, but he wasn't used to anyone in the shifter community being able to discern his innate magicality right off the bat. These two were unique in his experience. But then, he'd never really hung out with magic users before.

"My wife and I arrived this morning to help Belinda and hold down the fort until Grif and his brothers come to their senses." Keith spoke candidly as they all walked into a spacious living room. He too

11

looked fatigued, which was odd for a shifter. Most had vast reserves of energy and didn't tire easily. "I hope you have more success than I did. I spoke to Tim a few minutes ago. He called to see if you'd arrived and wants you to call him as soon as you have a sit rep."

Slade nodded. They all knew this situation was high priority for the Lords as well as everyone involved with Redstone Construction and the Cougar Clan. Slade wasn't surprised Tim would be checking on him even before he arrived, but he had to take stock of the situation first, before he'd have something to tell the Lords.

"Can you fill me in on what's been going on here?" Slade asked quietly. He'd learned over the years that a calm demeanor helped in situations like this. Not that he'd ever had so many lives riding on his shoulders as he did this time.

They all sat around a coffee table littered with maps and computer print outs. Slade would get to those in time, if they had a bearing on his investigation.

"Grif asked us to come," Valerie began. "We dropped everything and flew in this morning, to help with Belinda. It was bad enough losing her older sister a while back, but the poor child found her mother's body." Valerie's eyes grew suspiciously moist and her hand reached for her mate's.

The bond was strong between these two. Slade could almost feel the energy between them buzzing in the air — especially with the heightened emotion of the moment. This was a good partnership. Slade was almost in awe of how well their energies meshed.

But the news wasn't good. The youngest member of the family had to have been damaged emotionally by what she'd seen. No wonder the Clan was in such an uproar. Not only had they lost their matriarch, but the harm to the child was something that would haunt her throughout her life.

Slade had a great deal of sympathy for the child, but his mission was to stop the cougar Alpha from doing something that might bring further harm to his Clan, and everyone who worked for him. Slade had his work cut out for him.

"Can you give me any details of the attack?" Slade asked, not really hoping for much. These people had only arrived this morning. They were probably only a little more knowledgeable than he was on recent events.

Keith leaned back to unclip a cell phone from his hip. "I can't give you much, but I'll get my cousin here no matter how much he argues." He flipped it open and hit a speed dial number, a grim look on his face.

"Keith's cousins only waited for us to arrive and take charge of Belinda before they lit out of here, on the hunt. Personally, I'm glad you're here. Those guys aren't very rational right now from what little I saw."

Keith started talking to someone — arguing really — as the call connected and Valerie cringed, clearly embarrassed by the colorful language and heated exchange. Slade wasn't surprised in the least by the cougars' argument. He had assumed the Alpha and his brothers would be hotheads. This exchange only confirmed it.

"Sorry." Valerie gave him an uncomfortable smile.

"Don't worry," Slade answered. "I've heard worse."

Valerie laughed, her discomfort fading. "Yeah, I bet you have." She looked toward the staircase just visible through the arch they'd passed through to enter the living room. "Belinda is upstairs with—"

She was cut off as Keith swore and punched the end button on his phone.

"He's coming but he's not happy," Keith announced.

"Happiness is not required," Slade answered coolly as Keith eyed him.

"Oh, man. I'm not sure I want to be around to see this," Keith said with only a hint of humor.

Slade shrugged. "Stay or go. It doesn't really matter. Either way, I have a mission to accomplish."

The front door burst open and a ragged looking, sandy-haired cougar stalked in.

"Where is he?" the man roared before even clearing the doorway. He must've been nearby to have come so quickly. The door slammed shut behind him as he stomped into the living room.

Slade stood, ready for confrontation, his magic extending itself in a blanket of calm. It would do no good to fight with the cougar Alpha in his own home.

"I can help." He wanted that aspect of his presence to be abundantly clear. He didn't want to set himself up as the enemy from the get-go.

The Alpha paused in the archway, the magic hitting him, manipulating him just a tiny bit to help him calm. Valerie and Keith shot a look at Slade, but he ignored it. They could both sense his magic but the big, angry cougar in the archway didn't seem to notice. Slade counted on the other two to keep quiet about it as long as Slade didn't do anything to harm the other man.

"I'm Grif. Clan Alpha," he identified himself.

"I'm Slade. Tracker and head of security for the Lords. Thank you for returning to brief me, Alpha. I need every detail you have before I can get to work." Slade drew the man's attention to the coffee table and all the maps and print-outs. It seemed like Grif was calming enough to be sensible—at least for now.

Twenty minutes passed while Grif gave Slade every last detail he knew about the actual attack and everything else they'd been able to learn in the day since. The matriarch had been killed the day before, in her garden in back of the house. The youngest of the family had come downstairs to discover her mother's lifeless body in the backyard. The matriarch had been partially skinned in cougar form, which meant the killer had taken a piece of her pelt either as a trophy or as part of some kind of evil blood magic. Slade didn't like either option.

Since the killing, everyone had been on high alert. Grif had reached out to the Lords and his extended family. Many had answered his call. It became clear to Slade that this was an Alpha who was much loved by his Clan. Valerie and Keith kept their eyes on Slade throughout the conversation, clearly reserving judgment about his casual use of magic to calm the other man down.

"I need to see the spot where her body was found," Slade said at last, knowing the next few moments would be hard for the Alpha.

"There's nothing out there. The trail is cold. Not much in the way of clues. And the priestess took charge of my mother's body, thank the Goddess," Grif said in a low voice.

"Priestess?" That was the first Slade had heard of a priestess out this way, but he probably shouldn't have been surprised. Anyplace with this large a concentration of shifters was likely to attract Others of power as well. A priestess could be a good ally for this Clan.

"Kate," Valerie supplied, speaking for the first time since the Alpha had arrived. "She's upstairs with Belinda now. She has the most powerful healing gift I've seen in a long time, in addition to her other abilities."

"That's good," Slade nodded. "The little one will need her help."

"As will you." The strange female voice came from the archway.

Slade looked up to find the most beautiful woman he'd ever seen standing there, her gaze challenging him. Magic swirled around her. Green and gold, the color of sunshine and new growth. Healing and purification. This then, had to be the priestess, Kate.

Slade stood, unable to take his gaze from her.

The feminine vision strode forward, surety in her steps as she walked right up to Slade and held out her hand. He took her petite fingers in his much larger grip and was surprised by the strength with which she returned his gentle grasp.

The air of fragility about her was only an illusion. This woman had hidden depths and more power than he had ever encountered in a human. It tasted his magic where their hands met, swirling and twining up his arm before seeming to accept him. He realized in that moment she had tested him magically. He grinned at her audacity. Very few beings had ever challenged him in such a way. Usually, it annoyed him. Today, he found he liked it.

He extended his own magic the tiniest bit—just enough to let her know he knew what she'd done. He saw her eyes widen as his magic twined with hers, sealing their hands on more than just the physical level. Her gaze held his for a moment longer than was strictly polite and it seemed all in the room held their breath to see how this first meeting would go.

Kate blinked first, breaking the spell. She let go of his hand and he had no choice but to let her go as well. The magic between them unraveled and retracted, each to its owner.

"I'm Kate. Human, but a consecrated priestess of the Lady. Allie and Betina know I live here. You can check with them if you need someone to vouch for me."

"Your magic speaks for itself, milady." He dipped his head slightly, in respect, holding her gaze. "I'm Slade."

"Slade," she repeated his name as if tasting it, as their eyes held a beat too long. She shook herself and started back toward the archway. "We don't have time to waste," she said, changing tacks. "Come on. You need to see the garden."

"There's nothing out there—" Grif began in a tired voice but Kate cut him off.

"Nothing you can see. I think Slade will see a lot more. Accept his help, Alpha. The Lords sent him here for a reason. He's more than you know." Kate didn't wait but headed for the back of the house on light feet.

Slade made to follow her, but Grif held one arm out to bar his way.

"What does she mean? You're a cat, aren't you? You smell feline, but not cougar." Grif sniffed, testing the scent only another shifter could discern.

"Black leopard," Slade confirmed. Usually that was enough to satisfy other shifters. Leopards were scarce in this country, though they were beginning to make a bit of a resurgence.

"And more," Valerie stepped forward, as if daring Slade to deny what the magic users could sense in him. "Mage, but not. I've never encountered anything like you before, Slade. I admit, you're a puzzle."

Slade sighed. "I'm not a mage. I'm one hundred percent shifter. Mostly leopard but a few generations back in my ancestry there's something a bit rarer."

"What?" Grif demanded. "What are you that I should trust you?"

When he put it that way, Slade felt it only fair to answer honestly. Alpha to Alpha, he would give this man an answer to the question he never deigned to answer when asked by Others. This time, though, with this man, in this dire situation, he needed to be honest.

"I am snowcat," he admitted in a quiet voice.

"The most magical of shifters in the known world," Keith supplied in a low voice. "No wonder you light up our magesight like a firecracker. "And the way you sparked off the priestess..." Keith seemed to be thinking out loud. "Aren't snowcats holy men?"

"Tibetan mystics," Slade clarified. "They like to cultivate the myth that they're all the next best thing to a deity, but I'm proof they're merely mortal. More magical than most, but definitely mortal. My great-grandmother left Tibet centuries ago to travel the world with my great-grandfather. Theirs was a true mating." Slade looked down at the arm that still barred his path. "And now you know something about me that even the Lords don't know. I trust you'll keep it to yourselves. Anonymity is helpful in my line of work."

"You help me find the bastard that murdered my mother and I'll give you any damn thing you want. I'll keep your secret, as will my cousins. Right?" Grif looked at Keith and Valerie who both nodded solemnly.

"I'll find those who killed your matriarch and you will have justice for her death. This I vow," Slade replied.

"Then we have an accord." Grif moved his arm, offering his hand to seal the deal.

They shook hands and then all four of them walked out of the living room, heading down the hall toward the back of the house. They were following the young priestess who had missed their meeting of the minds. She waited for them in the backyard, chanting softly.

Slade felt the power of her magic the moment he stepped out of the house. She had lit up the area with magical energy.

Even from this distance, Slade could see the dark, roiling miasma of evil forces in one spot of the otherwise peaceful garden. He walked directly to it, knowing that was the spot where the matriarch had been slain.

"Stay here," Slade requested. "I'd like my first pass to be without your influence."

The cougars let him go while they watched from the deck.

"How does he know?" Grif asked his cousin. Slade could still hear them, but he was already on the trail.

"Kate lit the scene," Keith explained. "To someone with magesight, your backyard is filled with magical information. The spot where your mother... well... it's very obvious to me and my mate. To the leopard as well. And the priestess."

"Magic," Grif cursed. "It fouled the physical trail. None of us could find anything to follow."

"My money's on the leopard," Keith answered. "My magesight is good. Valerie's is better. But neither of us have the kind of skills the Lords hinted at this guy having. They sent him here for a reason. Our best bet is to let him do his thing, Grif."

Slade heard the answering growl of frustration from the Clan Alpha. He didn't blame the man. Slade would feel the same way if the roles were reversed. Shifters needed action. Sitting around letting someone else do the work went against the grain, but in this case, was necessary. Slade had the skills needed to unravel the magical trail that fouled the entire backyard. He'd done it before. He'd do it again.

Slade set to work, aware of the priestess, but she was good at keeping out of his way.

"You can see this, right?" Slade asked as he passed her in a neat row of tomatoes that had withstood the violence of the day before surprisingly well.

"I see it," she answered in a grim voice. This delicate woman had a core of steel, if he didn't miss his guess. She was holding up a lot better than he would have imagined, not shying away from the distasteful residual energies that littered the yard.

Slade stepped carefully, unraveling the energy trails left by the cougars who had taken away their matriarch's body and then scoured the yard looking for a physical trail. It was there, but there was no way the cougars could have seen it. Not without substantial magical help.

Even Keith and his mage mate would have trouble figuring this one out. Slade had seldom seen a more convoluted trail. He had no doubt it had been set up deliberately to foil pursuit. Whoever killed the matriarch had been concerned about shifters following them, but they'd also been aware of the magical friends the cougars could call on for help.

"Two of them did the deed," Kate whispered, her hands held aloft, using her magic to brighten the trails in a way Slade could not. But while she could enlighten, she didn't appear to be able to unravel them the way Slade could.

Her help was making this job easier than it would have been had Slade been attempting to read the energy trails on his own. For that reason—and to placate the restless cougars on the deck—he decided to humor her and speak his findings aloud.

"A man and a woman. The woman did the knife work," he confirmed, trying not to allow his disgust and anger rise too close to the surface. He needed to cultivate calm to do his work. That was often the hardest part of being who and what he was. The leopard wanted to rend and tear. The snowcat in him counseled for reason and measured justice. It was hard to reconcile.

"She follows the blood path," Kate confirmed, an ever-so-slight tremble in her voice. "They both do, but the male is the master in magic."

"The woman is the master in all other things. Killing, most of all," Slade confirmed, tasting the grass near the murder scene. It held the flavor of evil from the energies of those who had walked over it. The plants would recover with time as the magic dissipated and was cleansed by the innate energies of the earth, but for now, every living thing potentially held a trail he could follow.

"A deadly pair," Kate observed.

"I am deadlier." Slade stood and took a long look around the yard. Kate, wisely, made no comment to his soft-spoken statement.

CHAPTER TWO

"When will you begin the hunt?" Kate asked in a whisper as the most intimidating man she'd ever met stood so close, she could feel his body's heat.

"I already have." His haunting blue eyes shifted to her and she detected the faintest bit of humor behind his resolute gaze.

She admired that resolution and the deadly abilities she sensed in him. This was a man who had not lived a quiet life. No, even for a shifter, this Slade had lived a life of adventure, followed by purpose. She was able to sense that much about him.

That, and he was the absolute most devastating male she'd ever encountered. His magic tickled hers and had felt decidedly naughty when he'd let it out to twine up her arm during that handshake. One or two magic users had tried that trick in the past, but the feel of their power had always sickened her. Not so with Slade. No, with him, she wanted another taste, another tickle of his beguiling power.

Dangerous.

The man — shifter — was very dangerous to her both personally and in general. He was a killer, like most of his shifter brethren. A predator with a man's mind. A serious combination. But he was more. So much more. Magical and wild. Attractive and scary. A man of contrasts that drew her in as no man had ever done before. Not even that one, ill-fated relationship that had led her to where she was now.

Recalling that past mistake, she knew she would have to be careful around Slade.

But she also had a job to do. Like him, she'd promised her aid to the Cougar Clan and justice for the matriarch, a woman she'd both loved and respected. The matriarch had invited Kate into the community and made her welcome there, more than any other. Her death caused a deep pain of grief, but also the burning desire for justice. Maybe the shifter mentality was rubbing off on her, but Kate wouldn't rest until the killers had been dealt with. Only then would she allow herself to grieve for her lost friend.

"I can help," Kate offered, wanting to be part of the hunt as much as possible.

"You've done your part, Priestess. Thanks," Slade answered, already moving off toward the edge of the property, where it backed up onto scrub land that led into the desert. Kate followed, undeterred.

"I need to do more," she said stubbornly, putting her hand on his arm, stopping him in his tracks. "I've explored a lot since I got here. I know the desert around the housing development and how to navigate it safely." She knew she was daring greatly, but she had to be part of this. With that much magic at the killers' disposal, even this very magical werecat probably didn't stand a chance alone. "And I have experience with offensive magic. I've battled mages before."

One of his dark eyebrows rose in amusement at that last statement.

"All right," he conceded finally.

"I'm going with you," Griffon Redstone put in as he jogged silently across the big backyard.

Slade's gaze went to the big Alpha and then back to Kate. It was hard to tell his mood, but she saw definite amusement along with a hint of resignation in his glowing eyes.

"Now see what you've done?" he whispered in a low voice only the two of them could hear as he turned to face the approaching cougar.

"He would've followed you no matter what, and you know it," she whispered back, pleased to see an answering sparkle of amusement in his expression.

She would have said more but Grif stopped in front of them.

"What did you find?" the cougar asked in an almost angry tone. It was clear the Alpha didn't like not knowing.

Kate knew his moods well and decided to intervene. Sometimes cats liked to be smart asses for no apparent reason and she didn't want to chance this strange cat pushing Grif's buttons when he'd only just calmed down.

"Two killers," she said softly, in as calm a voice as she could muster, despite the anger and grief burning a hole in her gut. "A man and a woman. Both magic users following the blood path. The woman took the piece of your mother's pelt. I vow to you, Grif, I will get it back and lay your mother to rest with all the honor her bright spirit deserves." Kate stepped forward, tears held at bay through sheer force of will. "I will not rest until her spirit can be at peace."

"Thank you, Priestess," Grif said formally, though anger burned through the grief in his bloodshot eyes. "But the hunt is my right, as is the kill."

Slade held up his hands, palms outward, as Grif's steely gaze moved to him.

"You'll get no argument from me, Alpha. Yours is the kill, but in this case — with so much magic flying about — you definitely need my help to run them to ground."

"Mine too," Kate put in, not wanting to be excluded. "I can't kill, but I can damn well find them and hold them for you. Plus, depending on how far they've sunk into the blood magic, you may need me to purify them before they can actually die."

That was her ace in the hole. Without her abilities as a priestess of the Lady, they might not be *able* to kill their prey, even after they found it. Enabling the Alpha to get justice for his mother wasn't totally incompatible with her calling as a priestess, though she'd have to tread carefully. If the mages repented, the punishment for their crime would have to be less severe. But in her experience, once someone turned down the blood path, they didn't easily turn back to the Light.

"Which way did they go?" Grif asked Slade after a tense moment during which both men seemed to measure her words. Both wore hard expressions.

"Through the back gate and into the scrubland. I expect to find traces of a vehicle not too far from there — probably just out of sight of the house." Slade led the way as the two men strode for the gate that led out into the desert.

Kate followed right behind. She had to move fast to keep up with their long legged gaits, but she was used to being around shifters and was able to do a little skip-jog that helped her remain close to them without too much strain.

She kept her power up as she went, helping illuminate the trails that Slade followed. To her they were a confusing jumble of energy pathways that led off in all directions, but the tracker was showing his worth, leading them on a course that seemed clear in retrospect. Kate grew to respect his abilities to discern one life force from another. That was one powerful gift the strange cat had.

Griffon must have told the others to stay behind and guard Belinda. Kate was glad he was thinking clearly enough to realize his little sister might still be in danger. The fact that a blood path mage had taken a bit of the matriarch's fur was significant. Far more significant than the shifters might realize. Kate would make it her priority to impress upon the cougar Alpha what that meant in terms of magic for his people—and especially for his family. They were all in danger until that piece of their mother was reclaimed.

Slade led them out the back gate and into the desert beyond. There was sparse vegetation here and there. Occasionally there were rock formations. It was behind one of these that they found the tire tracks. A four by four of some kind. The men would know better than she what kind of vehicle made those tracks, she had no doubt.

"Long gone." Griffon spit in anger, pacing up and down around the tire tracks. Slade seemed content to let him work off some of his anger. Kate agreed with the strategy.

"Gone, but not forgotten," Slade countered a moment later, after he'd made a show of examining the scene from all angles. He'd also taken a photo of the tire impressions with his cell phone and punched a few buttons. Whether he'd sent it somewhere or fed it into a database, only he knew, but a moment later, he seemed to have a lot more information. "These tires are a new tread pattern. Very high end, but they come standard on the most recent luxury SUVs from these manufacturers." He showed what had to be a list on his phone to Griffon, who'd come to his side. "I've got a request out for a list of these vehicles in the area and their owners. That should help us narrow our search."

Griffon looked at Slade with new respect. "You have those kinds of connections to law enforcement?"

Slade nodded once. "I've lived most of my life in the human world. I had—still have—a job there. It allows me access to things and information barred from most others. In recent years, I've learned of the threat even greater than war among countries or terrorism. I've learned firsthand about the returning threat the *Venifucus* and their followers pose to all life in this realm. Once I understood that, I became more involved with shifter society and have offered my service to the Lords and all those on the side of Light. It's clear to me that what was done to your family is the work of evil. It's my vocation to fight it and gain justice for those harmed."

It was the most she'd heard from the tight-lipped shifter since they'd met and the speech impressed her greatly. She could literally see the glow of truth around him. He felt passionately about his profession and his vow to fight evil.

Kate could respect that. In fact, her opinion of the cat had just risen even higher than it had already been. By his words and actions—and especially his magic, which could not be faked to her senses—he'd shown himself to be one of the good guys. They were most definitely on the same side and any doubts she'd still harbored about him fled in the face of the undeniable truth in his words.

Griffon turned to fully face Slade and held out his hand. Slade took it and they shared a moment, the handshake joining them in the task ahead of them.

"Thank you for coming here to help us, Alpha," Griffon said firmly.

There it was. The acknowledgement that Slade was an Alpha—a leader in his own right. The fact that Grif openly acknowledged the other shifter's strength was a mark of respect. It placed them on equal footing, though Griffon was still the leader of his Clan and the wider grouping of shifters of all kinds that worked for him and followed his leadership.

"My skills are at your disposal, Alpha," Slade replied, just as meaningfully, "until justice has been served for your matriarch and your family, and all those who put their faith in you are safe from this threat."

Carefully worded, Kate noted, but such was the way with shifters. And with all magical folk, really. One had to be careful of exactly how much one promised, lest you end up beholden to another being of power for much longer than you ever intended.

29

"So what next? Where do you suggest we go from here?" The cougar Alpha actually deferred to Slade, which kind of amazed Kate. But it was a solid move. Slade clearly had more experience with this kind of thing than the businessman-builder.

"I think we should go back to the house and pick up my SUV. Then I want to come back around here by the nearest road and try to pick up the scent. By that time, the vehicle search will have spit back some possible matches. If the trail goes cold—which I expect to happen as soon as we hit a large road with lots of traffic—we can try to narrow down our list of suspect vehicles by triangulating from their last known location. Your people could help a bit with that, but I don't want any of them approaching the owners of the vehicles, just in case one of them is our perp. The two we tracked are too dangerous to be taken on by a lone shifter without magical support. But your Clan can help with surveillance. I know cougars are good at stealth." Slade gave Griffon the barest hint of a wry smile, which he returned, much to Kate's surprise.

The cougar Alpha had been alternately grim and irate since the death of his mother. It was good to see him focused and calm. Slade's influence and abilities had gone a long way toward helping the other cat regain some equilibrium. That alone was a gift from the Goddess. With Griffon calling for blood, his entire Clan had been more than a bit out of whack since the discovery of the matriarch's body.

Hopefully Slade could calm down the other Redstone brothers as easily. There was more than one hothead in the family.

When they arrived back at the family home a few minutes later on foot, having retraced their path through the backyard, Slade wasn't too surprised to find a few more cougars waiting for them. He remembered the background research on the family he'd read on the flight in.

The Alpha of the Clan was Griffon Redstone, the eldest of five brothers. All five were employed full-time in the family business except for the youngest, Matt. His background had piqued Slade's interest.

It was well known that Matt was close friends with several vampires who lived in the Napa Valley, including the Master of the region, a fellow named Marc LaTour. Slade knew Marc. They'd had some dealings a few years ago and Slade had liked the man… as much as he could like any bloodletter, at least.

It was Matt who bounded down the steps of the back deck to meet them as they walked through the garden, if Slade didn't miss his guess. The younger man went straight for his brother, clasping him in a hug that spoke of their shared grief and sorrow. Slade moved away, walking slowly with Kate as they both gave the brothers a moment of privacy.

"Matt must've just gotten home," Kate said softly. "He spends most of his time in California and I know the family was having a hard time getting a hold of him. Keith finally succeeded this morning, I believe." There were tears in Kate's pretty eyes as she spoke, but she steadfastly refused to let the tears fall. Slade admired both her strength and her compassion. It was a good combination to have in a priestess.

He reached for her hand, wanting to comfort her. It was an instinctual move and he only realized he'd done it when her eyes widened and her gaze sought his as her little hand slipped into his grasp. He'd caught her by surprise, it seemed. Could it be the priestess wasn't used to being touched? Curious.

He squeezed her hand, holding her gaze, wanting her to know that he understood both her sorrow and her surprise. Sorrow for the family that had lost its mother. Surprise for his reaching out to comfort her with even so simple a physical touch.

"Sounds like the rest of the family has gathered," Slade said, still holding her hand. He wanted her to become accustomed to his touch. He didn't ask why it suddenly seemed so important that she let him touch her. It just was.

He'd think about the implications later.

"You can hear inside the house?"

He grinned, not answering in words as he led her toward the back door.

"I'm going to have to remember not to talk to myself if I'm going to live among you guys." She shook her head and smiled as she preceded him into the house.

"You haven't lived around shifters before?" Slade's tone was conversational, but he had precious little information on the priestess.

Her file hadn't been among those given to him by the Lords and he was intrigued by the omission. He was also intrigued by the woman.

"Never. I was only just invited to move into this community recently. The new paint is barely dry on my living room walls yet," she joked. "And I still have a lot of painting and furniture moving to do. Not now, of course." She immediately sobered as they walked down the hall toward the living room. "This takes precedence over everything."

Slade was prevented from answering as they entered the living room. The large room was crowded now, big males—most with Alpha tendencies—filling the space with their presence. They all quieted as they saw Slade. His hackles went up, but he schooled himself to calmness. He had to show these other cats that he was in control.

Someone needed to be. It was clear these guys were in an uproar. There was a lot of angry energy in the room and one of the big men was pacing, stalking back and forth silently, menace and frustration clear in his every step.

Kate's steps hesitated only briefly before she strode into the center of the room. She was brave for a human, even if she was a priestess with strong mage powers. To face down a herd of angry cats in their very den took courage.

"Who's he?" One of the cougars sneered disrespectfully.

Keith was there and he stood, his hands out as he tried to calm the others.

"He was sent by the Lords," Keith explained. "He's got skills we don't. Be nice." Keith then turned to Slade and made the introductions. "Slade, these are my cousins, Steve, Mag and Robert." He pointed to each of the new cougars in turn.

One of the younger men reached out to shake Slade's hand. "Keith refuses to call me Bobcat. It started as a joke, but I like it. Thanks for coming out to help." He seemed to be the calmest of the Redstones.

Slade shook his hand and realized the man's outward calm was only an illusion. The tension in his grip indicated he was every bit as on edge as his brothers, but he was making an effort to hide it.

"I get it." Slade responded to the illusion of normalcy the cougar was trying to cultivate. "I have a werewolf friend whose human girlfriend nicknamed him Dawg, like that bounty hunter guy. The girl is long gone, but the nickname remains."

Robert chuckled and his brothers appeared to scoff, but the tension had eased in the room. It was slight, but it was an improvement.

"Gentlemen," Slade nodded to the other two, who still paced, though more slowly. "We found a trail that led out into the desert. It ended at vehicle tracks." Slade lifted his smartphone and hit a few buttons. "Based on the tread…" He read quickly through the report that had come in via his phone. "Well we got a bit of a break. The tire most likely belongs to a luxury import. Even though this town is known for high rollers, there aren't as many of these vehicles in the area as there could have been."

"How many?" Griffon asked from the entry to the living room. Slade had been peripherally aware of the Alpha and the youngest Redstone brother entering while he'd scanned the report.

"Less than a hundred," Slade replied, turning toward Grif. "Shouldn't be too hard to sniff them all out. I have a list of addresses, organized by area. If your men split up, they can each cover a sector."

"That'll be us," Grif said, eyeing each of his brothers as he spoke. "I assume you'll still be working on picking up the trail?" The look on Grif's face said

Slade damn well better still be working on that trail. Slade wasn't about to argue, since that had been his plan all along.

"Yes, Alpha. There are a few things still to do. I might be able to pick up the scent of their magic along the road and if that doesn't work, I have a few other tricks I can try to flush out their trail, while you and your brothers hunt the vehicle itself."

"One out of a hundred," Grif mused. "With five of us, that's about twenty addresses each. We all know the scents we're looking for and I don't trust anyone else to be as motivated as we are, right boys?"

The affirmations of assent were loud and quick. The brothers were definitely motivated to find their mother's killer.

"Keith," Griffon moved to stand in front of his cousin. "Your mission hasn't changed. There's nobody I trust more to watch over Belinda than you and your mate. I want you here, even though I know you'd probably rather be out there with us." Grif placed one hand on his cousin's shoulder and they shared a moment of silent communication.

"My priority is Belinda and my mate, Grif. Neither of them will come to harm on my watch."

"Good man," Grif clapped his cousin's shoulder and let go. "While you guard, the rest of us will go on the hunt." He turned to Slade expectantly.

They spent a few moments beaming the list to each other's smartphones and deciding who would take which sector. Slade admired the way they worked together. Like a well-oiled machine. Each brother seemed to have his own place within their family hierarchy and each had the respect of the others. It was nice to observe such a strong, well balanced group of men.

They were all Alpha in their own way, but they all deferred to Grif as their leader. In another family, such strong personalities might've led to argument and bloodshed, but this group had learned how to work together smoothly, respecting each other and helping each other rather than fighting amongst themselves.

"Kate and I will take my rental and check the desert. We might still be able to pick up the trail by either magical or mundane means," Slade announced.

"I'm going with you before I go hunting cars." Grif's tone brooked no argument. Slade could see the Alpha's mind was made up.

"All right," Slade answered slowly. He needed the Alpha to know that while he respected Grif's authority, the search was Slade's purview. A hard look passed between the men and Slade knew the message had been received. Not well, but it had been received. "Then we're all set," Slade said to the group at large as everyone started preparing to leave. "Check-ins every hour. When you complete your task, meet back here. Keith, can you or Valerie man the phone, coordinate and keep track of everyone while guarding the child?"

"Can do," Valerie chimed in from the entry to the living room. She walked over to her mate and smiled softly up at him.

Keith Redstone nodded, putting his arm around his wife's shoulders. Their magical skills were best suited to keeping the homestead and the traumatized girl safe. Slade might need their help later, but for now, this was the best place for them.

"I'll keep a roster, gather data, if any, and pass it along to you every hour or sooner, if there's need," Valerie confirmed. It sounded like she was more than capable of lending a hand to this effort.

Slade nodded his thanks and the impromptu meeting broke up, everyone heading out in different directions. This was a lot more help than he usually had on his missions and he was glad of it, even if not all of the cougars could be trusted to keep a lid on their tempers. He'd have to watch them all closely—especially as they drew closer to their prey.

He didn't want anyone else dying on his watch. Or worse.

CHAPTER THREE

Grif sat up front with Slade in the rented SUV. Kate took the back seat as they pulled away from the cougar homestead. Slade wasn't sure why the Alpha had decided to tag along rather than get his part of the vehicle hunt under way as soon as possible, but there had to be a reason. This Alpha was a good one. Very deliberate and very powerful. He didn't have dominion over just his family or just his Clan, but over a far-reaching collection of shifters of all kinds who worked for his company and followed his leadership.

Next to the Lords, Griffon Redstone was probably the most powerful Alpha in the States.

"You carry yourself like a Teams guy, but somehow I doubt that was your path." There it was. The reason Grif had wanted to talk to him. The Alpha wanted to know where Slade had come from—his background and qualifications.

"Nah, I'm not a Navy cat," Slade admitted. He didn't mind talking about his past in the military to Grif. Slade had read his file. He knew Griffon Redstone and his brother Steve had been Special Operators. Army Green Berets, in fact. It was a small community and Grif probably knew every shifter in the Berets and quite a few of those who had been SEALs, but he couldn't place Slade yet and that probably bothered him. Slade understood. "Marine Force Recon." Slade solved the mystery. "Mostly I served in Asia because of my talent with the languages of that region and my ancestry. My great-grandmother was born and raised in Tibet and I picked up a lot from her."

Grif looked over at him. Slade could feel the other man's scrutiny but he was concentrating on the road. He'd already told the Alpha more than most people knew. That was as far as he was willing to go at the moment.

No doubt Grif had his suspicions. All shifters had heard about the weirdness in Tibet and the strange tales that originated there. It was an exotic land full of mystery and intrigue, both in the human world and in the world of the *were*.

"Recon, eh?" Grif said after a while, no doubt getting the message that Slade would go only so far in revealing his past to a relative stranger—even one as highly placed as Griffon Redstone. "You were tapped by the Company, weren't you? That's why you're off the grid and still connected to the game."

"You're no fool, Alpha," Slade said by way of answer.

He wouldn't come straight out and say he still occasionally did work for the CIA, but if Grif figured it out on his own, he wasn't going to try to mislead the man either. The Lords knew and the fact that he worked for Uncle Sam when called, wasn't something he needed to hide from Grif or the Lords. It wouldn't be good if it became public knowledge, but certain people in the *were* hierarchy probably needed to know. Slade had just decided Grif was part of that select group.

Kate too, though Slade didn't have a good reason to let her in on his secrets other than the belief that she could be trusted and he wanted her to know more about him. His attraction to the priestess was making him incautious, but he was following his instincts where she was concerned. All he could do was pray to the Lady they both served that his instincts wouldn't lead him astray in the case of the all-too-attractive priestess.

Slade lapsed into silence as he concentrated on driving. Grif had apparently been satisfied by his revelations and let the matter drop for now.

Slade lowered the window as they approached the area where the trail had gone cold. Grif followed suit. Both took a deep breath, but it was Slade who picked up on the magical probes coming from the backseat. He caught Kate's eye in the rearview mirror and winked. The cats would look for scent. The mages would look for magic. Only Slade could do both simultaneously.

It was a trick that had stood him well in the past. Hopefully the combination would be enough to sniff out the trail this time too.

Kate was a distraction, to be sure, but he was glad she was along on this particular op. She had skills in addition to being the prettiest partner he'd ever had on a mission.

"Stop the car." Kate's voice sounded strained and only then did Slade stop thinking about the woman and start concentrating on the task at hand.

He should've noticed it before she did. There was magic afoot here. Very close. And very dark.

"What?" Grif asked, scenting the wind with a scowl on his face even as Slade pulled the vehicle over to the side of the road and parked.

"Magic," Slade answered, already sending his senses outward, trying to figure out how best to approach. The magical indicators were growing weaker, but they were definitely there.

All three of them got out of the SUV. Kate and Slade took the lead as Grif brought up the rear. Kate did her thing and the scene lit dramatically with a few waves of her hands and a low-voiced chant.

"I see it," Slade murmured, knowing his companions would hear him. He moved off in the direction of the trail.

He could see now where the trail had been masked at the point they lost it earlier. Very nearby, it crossed the road and began again, much more faintly. Apparently the killers could hide completely on the asphalt of the road, but something about the desert held the last little glimmers of dark power that had traversed it.

"The land didn't like them," Kate whispered, almost as if to herself. "We're seeing the trace of its rejection of their attempts to hide themselves." She looked over at Slade and they shared a moment of silent communication.

It was almost as if he could hear what she was thinking. This land was sacred. Kate, as a priestess, had probably done ceremonies in and around the shifter housing development, including this patch of desert, to consecrate the lands to the Lady. It was a form of protection she probably did as a matter of course whenever she moved to a new place.

That simple act had allowed them to follow the trail that otherwise probably would have remained hidden.

Grif cleared his throat behind them, breaking the spell. Kate jumped a bit but Slade hid his reaction better, merely turning to nod at the impatient Alpha who was following them. Grif would have been within his rights to voice his objection to the delay a little more vocally, but he was being polite.

"Sorry," Kate murmured. She fell back to explain what was going on to the cougar as Slade forged ahead, walking carefully to avoid disturbing the fragile trail.

He followed it for some time, more than a hundred yards from where they'd found it again. He thought they might really be on to something when the trail just... petered out.

"That's it." Slade said after his third loop around, looking for the remnants of the trail. He threw his hands up in disgust. "Kate, do you see anything more?"

She shook her head. "No, sorry."

"What are you saying?" Grif asked in a quiet voice as if he was trying really hard to keep himself calm.

"The trail ends here." Slade faced the cougar Alpha, not backing down from Grif's very obvious, frustrated anger.

"Ends?" Grif growled.

"Yes, Alpha." Slade spoke firmly, but respectfully, acknowledging their respective ranks. "I will try to find it again, but it could take quite a while and I can't promise I'll find the scent again. For now, this is as far as I can take you."

The growl continued as Grif paced away, clearly upset. A moment later, he turned on his heel and strode back, appearing to come to a decision.

"All right then. You keep working on this. Call in when you have something to report. Kate, you want to come back with me or stay here?"

"I'll stay and work with Slade. Maybe together we can find it again." Something indefinable made her want to stay with the mysterious shifter. They all walked quickly back to the SUV. They'd need it to resume their work farther up the road.

"I'll run back," Grif decided swiftly and began to strip as they neared the vehicle.

In deference to Kate, no doubt, he moved behind the rental car to get completely naked. He made a ball of his clothing and chucked it into the back of the rented SUV before shifting to his cougar form and taking off at a fast lope, straight across the scrubby desert. He'd be back to his family home in no time.

"So what now?" Kate turned to face Slade.

He held her gaze for a beat too long before replying and she wondered what was going through his mind. "Normally, I'd prowl, but not with you in tow. Two feet aren't as fast as four."

"Are you saying I slow you down?" She shifted her weight to one side and crossed her arms in challenge.

"You can't deny that you do, but I need your skills."

"Oh, that's nice." His tone annoyed her.

Perversely, she wanted him to want her around for more than just her magical skills. She'd only known him for a few hours and already her mind was running to places it was better off not straying. They had a job to do. That was all. It was unlikely a guy like him would be interested in her. Better to not even think in that direction.

"Simple truth." He shrugged. "I don't expect you're the kind of woman who tolerates lies, even polite ones." Now he was challenging her. It felt like banter and there was a definite light of attraction in his eyes. Maybe she wasn't the only one thinking in dangerous directions.

Rawr.

"You're very blunt."

"Nature of the beast, I'm afraid." He smiled to soften his words as he began moving slowly toward the vehicle. She followed his lead, curious. "We'll take the SUV and sniff around magically. Cover more ground that way. We might have a shot at finding *something*."

"But you don't really think so, do you?"

"Frankly, no. These guys are too good. I'm surprised we even got this far."

So was she, but she wasn't going to say it out loud. They needed a break. They needed to find the trail again. She would not rest until they found something and she didn't want to say anything negative that might jinx their path.

"We'll find it. I know we will." Kate sent up a silent prayer as she walked beside Slade to the SUV.

He opened the passenger door for her and she tried to enter the vehicle, but he blocked her path, caging her between the open door, the vehicle and his big, hard body. Kate looked up into his eyes, surprised by his sudden move.

"What?" she whispered, unsure of his motives. Could he really be as attracted to her as she was to him?

A rumble of sound, barely perceptible from his throat was her only answer as his head dipped. His lips drew close to hers, passing over once, twice, touching lightly at first, as if testing the texture and shape of her mouth.

She needed more. Oh, so much more.

Kate lifted upward, millimeter by millimeter, closer to his warm body, his surprisingly gentle kiss. Moment by moment, she increased the pressure between their lips. She was surprised he was allowing her to control the kiss. He'd seemed more the type to take what he wanted than to seek permission.

Although… he wasn't exactly asking permission. It was more like he was seducing her into her own downfall. By making her seek his kiss, he brought her to him, a willing victim, giving up all control to the master.

And there was nothing she wanted more at this moment than to have him deepen the kiss. She wanted to taste his essence and learn the pleasure she suspected only he could bring her. She thought she might not ever be the same.

Then he really kissed her. He turned the tables, wrapping his arms around her and pulling her close. He deepened the connection, running his tongue along her lips until she surrendered and opened to him.

It was divine. Her temperature soared as his body enveloped hers and he took total control of the kiss and her pleasure. He was the master of her fate for those stolen moments that burned hotter than the desert sun.

And it was only a kiss. As devastating as it was, he kept it simple and to his credit, he didn't try to push her beyond a kiss into something even more dangerous. Not at first, anyway.

She moaned a little as his arms tightened around her. She felt motion and then the hard panel of the back door of the SUV up against her back. His arms formed a cage around her, keeping her in place, but to be honest, she wouldn't have moved away from him if given the chance. Wild horses couldn't drag her away from Slade's arms. Not now. Maybe not ever.

Her leg rose almost involuntarily, sliding along the outside of his as he stepped closer. He fit perfectly against her, even though he was so much taller than she. Somehow it worked. Masculine hardness to feminine yielding. She slid her hands upward, over his chest, loving the feel of him against her palms.

She wanted more. So much more.

The kiss went on and when he finally dragged his mouth from hers, she was gasping for air. Her body trembled as his lips trailed down her neck, biting gently on the skin just under her ear. It was the most delicious sensation she'd ever felt. She wanted it to go on forever.

And then the phone rang.

Actually, it beeped. Slade's cell phone beeped incessantly, demanding attention.

He cursed under his breath, his head dipped over hers, bent as he drew in deep breaths. She was mollified to see he'd been as lost in the moment as she.

"I've got to take this," he whispered, reaching for the phone clipped to his belt.

Slade eased away from her, touching the screen of the small phone and answering with a single, impatient word. He walked a few feet away, moving slowly as she just leaned against the SUV and tried to catch her breath.

Damn. The guy was potent. She'd forgotten everything in his embrace. The matriarch. The sorrow of the family. The dire situation. Their mission to find the trail.

Everything had become unimportant when Slade held her in his arms. The only thing that had mattered was the taste and feel of him. The way he touched her and seduced her senses. The way he made her feel.

Thinking had been beyond her for those stolen moments, but she couldn't let it happen again. At least not until they'd solved the problem facing the cougars. She was sworn to aid the shifter community that had adopted her and she would do all in her power to help find the matriarch's killers. She couldn't let Slade—scrumptious as he was—distract her from her task.

After they'd found the killers and the crisis had been dealt with... maybe then there might be time for her desires. If Slade stuck around. For all she knew, he'd do his job and leave, never to be seen again.

That thought finally made her move. She straightened from her boneless lean against the car and sat down in the front passenger seat. She buckled in as Slade talked in short, brisk sentences to whoever had interrupted their moment alone.

She should be thankful they'd been interrupted. She'd been *that* close to ripping his clothes off and having her way with him right there in the desert. Not normally the kind of behavior she engaged in, but this man was proving special in many different and exciting ways.

She watched him move, her eyes undeniably drawn to his tall, lanky form. He was without doubt one of the most impressive men she'd ever come across—and that included all her recent exposure to the amazingly handsome shifters that worked for Redstone Construction.

If she'd simply wanted a bed partner, she could've given the signal to any one of the good looking studs who lived in the housing development, but she hadn't been interested. Not in any of them. They were fun to look at, of course, but she hadn't felt a spark from any of the men she'd met in the past few months. Heck, not even in the past few *years.*

Not only did she feel sparks from the mysterious Slade, she'd felt outright lightning bolts of the most delicious kind when he'd taken her in his arms and taken control of that kiss. He knew what he was doing when it came to women, of that she was certain. But was she just a passing flirtation while he was in town? Or had he felt the same instant attraction when they'd first met?

Was she the only one drawn against their better judgment into a situation that she neither had the time, nor the courage for? He was scheduled to leave once he'd finished his work here. His life was elsewhere. He worked for the Lords and probably lived up in Montana, near them.

She just didn't see how this situation could end well if she took that irrevocable step and gave into the attraction any more than she already had. She'd wind up with a broken heart. And would the mysterious cat shifter even think of her after he was gone? Sadly, she thought not.

Better to focus on the task at hand. That phone call couldn't have happened at a more opportune moment. She needed to get her mind off of his handsome, hard body and back on the mission. She'd promised to help find the murderers and she had already been able to help. She felt pride in the fact that her magic had enabled Slade to track them this far.

Together, perhaps they could pick up the trail again and find those responsible for sending the entire shifter community in the Southwest into an uproar. The Redstone matriarch had been well loved.

Kate had been impressed by the older woman. Grif's mother had been the first one to extend the invitation to Kate to join the community. She'd taken Kate under her wing and helped her figure out her place in the group. Or at least, she'd begun to do that. And then she'd been brutally murdered.

Kate had lost a champion among the *were* with whom she'd chosen to live. But much more importantly, she'd lost a friend. A tear came to her eye when she allowed herself to think of the kind woman who'd taken her in and made her feel welcome. So few times in her life had she felt that way, and Kate knew she was going to miss the matriarch of the Redstone Clan as much those who had known that brave lady much longer. She'd been that kind of woman. She'd made an indelible impression on the lives of everyone she knew.

Slade ended the call, putting the phone away, and strode around to the driver's side of the vehicle, a determined expression on his face. Would he now tell her their brief moment of passion had been a mistake? She didn't want to hear it, even if she was beginning to believe that herself.

"Matt picked up the scent," he said instead, surprising her and deferring the dreaded post-kiss conversation to sometime in the future. Thank goodness.

Slade slipped behind the wheel and closed the door, starting the SUV almost all in one motion. He moved fast. Shifters had incredible speed, agility and strength, she was coming to learn. Slade, perhaps, was even a bit sharper than the others she'd come to know.

"Are you up for the hunt?" The look in his eyes dared her to join him.

She felt her resolve firm as she thought again of the matriarch.

"I'm up for it," she replied in kind, already looking forward to helping Slade find out all he could from the trail. Whatever — or whoever — it led to.

CHAPTER FOUR

"What did Matt say on the phone?" Kate asked as they got back on the road.

Slade had to get his head back in the game. For a moment there, all he'd wanted to do was ignore the phone—ignore his duty—and sink into Kate's luscious body. She was dangerous to his peace of mind, never mind his work.

"Actually, it was Valerie. She's coordinating the messages. Matt called her first, but I don't trust him not to call Grif next. Unless we get there fast, we're going to have a family of irate cougars raining hell down on whoever owns that vehicle, whether or not they're the ones we're looking for."

This was a tricky part of their mission. Slade had been sent to defuse the Redstones. To run interference so they didn't do something in their rage and grief to expose the entire shifter community to the human world. The secret must be kept. And Slade had to be the one to make certain of it. The Redstones weren't clear headed enough at the moment to think before they acted.

"I'm surprised Matt even bothered to call at all before rushing in where angels fear to tread," Kate offered.

"He's pegged as the maverick of the family, from all accounts," Slade agreed. "But he also seems more level headed than his years would indicate. Maybe he's just used to following orders from having so many older, Alpha siblings."

"I thought only Grif was the Alpha. How can there be more than one?"

The question, so innocent yet so blind, made Slade realize just how clueless Kate still was about his world, priestess or not. She may know about magic and the human world, but she didn't seem to know the first thing about shifters.

"Every male in that family has Alpha tendencies. Any one of them could make a bid to rule over their Clan and the extended, mixed group of shifters that work for Redstone Construction. But Griffon is the eldest. He was the one who built the business and attracted so many other shifters to work for him and follow his lead. He's the clear leader of that family. The other brothers seem to accept that and curb their own Alpha tendencies somewhat, out of love and deference to their brother." Slade turned the SUV onto the highway and sped up, hoping to get to Matt before the brothers gathered. "I've seen it go the other way too. Less kind Alphas with Alpha siblings have been torn apart by their younger family members in the worst cases. In other situations, the younger brothers are a thorn in the sides of their elders. A lot of times, the younger brothers go off and form their own small Packs or Clans."

"They can just do that? Move away and start over?"

"Yeah. Sometimes it's the only choice. Starting a Clan from scratch isn't easy, but there are always loners out there, looking for a home or a leader — or both. It's a bit easier for cats than wolves. Wolves need tighter community bonds, in general. Cats often go their own way and tend to need their space and time alone every once in a while. We need to prowl."

"I get that. Humans do too, sometimes," she said softly, almost contemplatively. Slade spared her a glance and she was looking out the window with such a forlorn expression that he wanted to reach out and touch her, to bring her focus back to him and away from whatever brought such sorrow to her beautiful face.

"Is that why you're out here, roughing it among shifters?" He asked his question in a low, gentle, coaxing voice. If she wanted to talk, he wanted her to know he was more than willing to listen.

Her gaze met his as her head turned. She gave him a puzzled smile that was faint, but much better than the melancholy she'd been displaying.

"I'd hardly call that luxurious house they gave me *roughing it*." She chuckled softly. "But yeah, in a way, I guess you could say I've always been a loner, as you put it. The odd man out, so to speak. You see, my parents died when I was very little. I was raised in foster care for the most part." The admission seemed a big one for her, so he didn't reply, just let her say what she wanted to say. He wouldn't push her. He wanted her to open up on her own — or not. The choice had to be hers. "My foster parents didn't really understand me. I always saw the world a little differently than everyone else, and when the magic began to emerge..." she trailed off, her gaze dropping to her lap, drawing inward.

"They didn't know a damn thing about magic, did they? Probably didn't believe in it and couldn't sense the energy patterns in the world around them. Am I right?"

The highway stretched and they were moving as fast as Slade dared push the vehicle without running afoul of law enforcement. But inside the rented SUV, the moment was quiet... intense. Emotions ran high from the little woman sitting at his side. He wanted to take her into his arms and comfort her with his touch, but maybe it was better he couldn't. Like a lost little kitten, he had to let her come to him — verbally, emotionally, and ultimately, physically. If they got that far.

And the Goddess knew, he wanted to get that far — as far as Kate would let him go. He wanted her, and if fate was kind, he'd have her in his bed before he left Nevada.

"They weren't bad people. They just didn't understand me. I can't blame them, really. I don't understand myself half the time." She smiled faintly, ruefully. "I searched for a long time before finding someone who knew what magic was and was willing to help me. It didn't turn out the way I expected, but at least it set me on the path."

Slade sensed turmoil from her as she thought about her past. He *had* to reach out this time, placing one hand over hers on the console between them. That simple action drew her gaze as their energies met and twined together the tiniest bit, as if offering comfort.

"The first magic user I met tried to trick me. Actually, he *did* trick me. I'm not too proud to admit it. I was a fool. I got used and abused and it almost destroyed me both emotionally and magically." She pulled her hand out from under Slade's and turned to look out the window again.

If she could have, he imagined she would have rolled up into a fetal ball. As it was, both hands clutched her stomach as if pain lingered. The guy, whoever he was, must have really hurt her.

Slade wanted to kill him. Plain. Simple. Black and white. Slade wanted the bastard dead, his blood pooling out under Slade's claws.

Whoa, boy.

Slade wasn't entirely successful in suppressing his growl. It rumbled through the small cab of the SUV, low and deadly before he could stop himself.

Kate looked over at him, surprise in her gaze, but no fear. "It's really okay, Slade. He's long gone and I learned a valuable lesson from him. Nobody ever took advantage of my naiveté like that again. And they never will." Her mood switched from victim to victor in that moment and Slade calmed.

She had become stronger as a result of her life experience. He would have spared her the bad times if he could, but at least she had learned from them. Not everyone was so lucky. Many people had to repeat the mistakes over and over before they evolved—if they ever did.

"So what's the story? Did you fall for a guy who only wanted you for your power?" He didn't *want* to know, but perversely *needed* to know the details.

This little priestess was beguiling him. Making him want things he'd never really wanted before. He wanted to know what made her tick, and all about her past. That wasn't something he generally cared about when he was attracted to a woman. Usually, the less he knew about a bed partner, the better. But not so with Kate.

She fascinated him in many different ways. The taste of her magic, the strength of her power, the beauty of her spirit and the lovely package that wrapped all of it—those things only hinted at the core of the woman beneath. And he wanted to know all about her. What made her the way she was and where she'd come from. The paths she'd walked before meeting him and what they had done to her.

Slade almost shook his head at his own thoughts. Was he becoming sentimental in his old age? Probably not, but this reaction was definitely a change for him. Something about this priestess brought out more than just his protective side. She inspired feelings he'd never really experienced before in conjunction with a woman he wanted to fuck so bad, his eyes nearly crossed.

And the need for her was only growing stronger as they talked, not weaker. In the past, when a woman started unloading the baggage of her past on him, Slade's interest would quickly wane. Not with this woman. No, the more she revealed, the more he wanted to know.

It was something to ponder. Later. First he wanted to hear more about the man who'd almost broken her.

And he wanted most especially to know the bastard's name so he could hunt him down and...

"Wayne was older than me. Not a lot older, just enough to make him seem more worldly and interesting to a twenty year old who had little experience with men. He was charming and urbane and within six months of meeting him, I'd moved in with him."

"How did you meet?" Slade ruthlessly suppressed his desire to growl in both anger and triumph. He'd learned the man's first name. He only needed a little more to track him down.

"He was a research assistant at the university I attended. He was working on his Ph.D. while I was a shy undergrad. He knew about magic. He was the first person I'd ever met who understood the energies I'd been seeing and manipulating all my life."

"So he became your mentor in magic as well as your lover?" Slade wanted to claw something, but held the anger in. It wouldn't do to scare her. Not when she was just opening up to him.

"Something like that. I didn't realize until about six months later that he was slowly siphoning off my power. He was a magical parasite. He was growing stronger while I was getting weaker."

"A magical vampire?" Slade asked, surprised. He'd never really heard of such a thing, but he supposed it was possible.

"Yeah. A vampire. That's a good word for him, though not the bloodletting kind. This guy was more like the old horror movie bad guys." She sounded bitter and more than a little angry. Good for her. She still had some spirit after what had been done to her.

"You thought he loved you?" Slade asked in a quiet voice.

"Oh, yeah. I bought his act hook, line and sinker. All he really wanted was to drain my power and make himself even stronger."

"How'd you make the break?"

"I didn't let on that I realized what he was doing. I'd been suspicious, but I didn't really know for sure until I had a little magical breakdown one day. It was as if I was blind to the magical world. I couldn't sense anything. Not the green light and song of the trees or the golden pulse of the earth. All my magical senses were gone. That's when I finally realized the extent of what he'd done to me. I packed my stuff when he was working and took off."

"You lost your ability to sense magic?" He was shocked she'd been through so much. "How did you evade him if you couldn't sense him coming? I assume he tracked you?"

"Yeah, he tracked me. But during our relationship, there was one place he refused to allow me to go. There was a little spot up in the woods above campus. It was a stone circle. It was sort of infamous among certain student groups. It was rumored some of the goth kids would go up there on the full moon and party, though I never really saw any evidence of it. I'd wanted to investigate it, but Wayne refused to let me go near the site. He told me it was an evil place and that I'd die if I went up there. When I ran for it, I figured if he'd been lying to me about everything else, that had to be wrong too. So I hiked up there with my little knapsack full of all my worldly possessions, sat down in the center of the stone circle and cried my eyes out."

He reached out to her again, placing one hand on her arm. She didn't move away and he stroked her skin gently, offering what comfort he could while still driving safely down the highway. They were getting close to their objective, but he wanted to hear the rest of her tale. He was feeling more than a little torn between duty and his desire to comfort the incredible woman he'd discovered.

"How did you get away from him? He must have found you up there, right?" Slade could guess how the story went, but he wanted to hear it from her.

"He came to the circle, but he couldn't enter. He prowled around the perimeter alternately whining and shouting, berating me. Calling me a stupid cow. Then he'd be cajoling, trying to get me to come back to him. Fat chance." She made a rude sound and Slade felt a smile coming on. She had spirit and he discovered he'd like that in a woman. "Night fell and I didn't realize it then, but it was the sabbat of Imbolc."

"February," Slade realized. "I hope you went to school in the south."

His attempt at levity seemed successful. She turned to him and smiled. "Texas A&M," she replied. "It was chilly, but not freezing."

"And since you were in a stone circle on Saint Brighid's Day, I'm guessing at some point somebody showed up. Shifters? A priestess or two? A coven of witches?" he teased.

"Remember those goth kids I mentioned? Well, they weren't just goth. They were werewolves. And one of the philosophy professors was a priestess. She was an older lady, gray haired and sort of sturdy, of German background. She huffed and puffed her way up that hill and found Wayne there, berating me. I was still in tears, a mess from what he'd done and the things he'd been saying since he showed up at the stone circle. She was having none of it. She tapped her walking stick on the ground and that's when Wayne got his first taste of *real* power. Me too, actually. The magic came flooding back as the pathways inside me that had been starved were suddenly filled. I stopped crying and watched her take Wayne down a peg or two while the wolves ranged around her protectively. He was totally outclassed and outnumbered, but he still didn't leave."

"He didn't want to give up his juicy prize," Slade said, disgusted with the other man.

"Too right," Kate agreed. Her voice was stronger now as she remembered the moment she had broken free of Wayne's hold over her. "I stood up and began speaking. I told him off at first and then, it was like something took me over, and I cursed him, dispersing his power and sending it back to Mother Earth. I had no idea where that came from. I'd never done such a thing before, but I think the Goddess spoke through me on that special night, while I was standing in that sacred place. She worked through me to stop Wayne's evil."

"You became a priestess that night, didn't you?" Slade asked, intrigued by the idea. He'd never heard of such a unique experience. Kate was proving herself to be special in many different ways.

"Yeah, by accident, I guess, but it was the best *accident* I've ever been in. It changed my life. It impressed the heck out of Hilda and the wolves. They took me in, though I think they were always a little afraid of me after that. I spent the next two years with them as I finished my degree and learned about being a priestess from old Hilda. The wolves were friendly after that, but not gushingly so. They protected me. And Wayne was run out of the university—out of the state, even. They hustled him out of there so fast, I think his head is still spinning." She laughed for the first time since starting her sad tale. "The wolves keep tabs on him, just in case. For my part, I'll be happy if I never see his sorry face ever again."

Slade felt satisfaction rumble through him at her words. Good. She was over the other man and didn't want anything to do with him. She'd had her closure and was content to let others handle the follow up. To him, that was a good sign.

"Where did you go after that?" Slade wanted her to keep talking. He wanted to know everything she was willing to tell him about her past.

"Hilda had some friends up north. I apprenticed with two priestesses in Indiana for a few years, then moved to Missouri to learn more from a solo priestess who needed some help. She was being overrun by magic users who wanted control of the stone circle she guarded. They weren't evil, just misguided, and there was a bit of a turf war going on until I showed up as reinforcement. I've always been pretty good at offensive magic—ever since what happened with Wayne, at least—so Allie and Betina send me in where there's a problem. This is the first peaceful assignment I've been given, actually," she reflected.

"Not so peaceful now, though, is it?" Slade took the exit he needed off the highway and began to navigate the smaller streets. They were close now.

"The Lady moves in mysterious ways. The High Priestess couldn't have known what was going to happen, but maybe she had a feeling that I needed to be here. Who knows? At this point, I'm just glad I'm here to help."

"Me too," Slade admitted.

He hadn't been expecting to have a partner on this mission, but he found himself glad Kate was around and able to illuminate the magical path. That was something he couldn't do on his own and he was man enough to admit that he wouldn't have gotten this far on the trail without her.

Slade usually worked alone. He'd spent decades perfecting his skills and the few times he had tried to work with a partner had been lessons in frustration. Not so, this time. He was rapidly discovering he not only liked having Kate around, but she was damn useful when it came time to track.

"Thanks." She smiled at him and he felt his heart lift.

Slade turned the vehicle, shattering the moment as they arrived at their destination. She had no idea why she'd opened up to him the way she had. Normally, she was very reticent to speak about her past with anyone. Something about Slade appealed to her on many different levels, and he'd turned out to be a good listener. Who would have guessed it?

She felt more comfortable with him than she had with any shifter. Actually, she felt more comfortable with him, than she had with any*one*. Ever. It was like they were kindred spirits. She wanted to know his story too—especially after spilling her guts to him about one of the most painful experiences in her life.

But there wasn't time. Not now.

No, now they had to sort out a bunch of irate cougars and get to the bottom of a murder so heinous, it had half the shifters in the country up in arms. On a personal level, Kate wanted justice for her friend, the matriarch. And she wanted to help protect the shifters she had come to know and care for here in Nevada.

Slade handled the vehicle expertly, rounding curves with ease at a higher speed than she would have been comfortable driving at. She trusted his skills and reflexes, though, and felt secure with him at the wheel.

They were moving into an outlying part of the city, where McMansions popped up out of the desert. She looked more closely. These were older homes, possibly from the last failed housing boom and many of them hadn't been kept up the way they should have been. They looked old and a few they passed were in rather obvious disrepair, or looked abandoned.

"This was one of those developments that failed after the housing bubble popped," she observed. She'd learned quite a bit about the housing and construction market since joining the Redstones in Nevada.

"Most of these were probably foreclosed, or the owners lost a lot of equity after buying," Slade agreed, navigating the twining streets of the development.

She felt it before she saw it. The tingle of dark magic alerted her even before they turned the corner. She grabbed Slade's arm and he immediately slowed.

"Feel it?" She was unable to speak above a whisper. Her blood chilled at the evil that was only growing stronger.

"Yeah." His tone was grim as he answered her.

Slade pulled the SUV over to the curb between houses. These once-luxurious homes were spaced out and had a lot of vegetation between them for privacy. Palms and giant cacti interspersed with lots of ground cover made a convenient landscape for them to sneak up on the house that was the center of the evil energy.

Slade got out of the SUV, moving silently. Kate did her best to follow suit, but it wasn't easy to operate as quietly as a cat. Still, she did her best, walking around the back of the vehicle to follow in Slade's tracks.

The light was beginning to fade. They'd been tracking for far longer than she thought. Only the granola bar in her pocket, quickly gobbled after her stomach started to grumble hours earlier, had kept her going.

But hunger was the last thing on her mind. She was too keyed up to worry about such a trivial thing at the moment. Evil was pulsing through the pavement, through the earth. *Unpleasant* didn't begin to describe the sensations she was experiencing as the good earth rejected yet wasn't strong enough to overpower the evil rolling over it. She felt nausea rise in the pit of her stomach, but pushed it down as best she could.

"Stay close. The cougars are nearby." Slade fell back to whisper near her ear.

Sure enough, as they came even with the largest bird of paradise plant she'd ever seen, Matt and his brother Robert were waiting on the other side, well hidden by the shade of the enormous plant.

"Anybody else get here yet?" Slade asked, joining them. He included Kate in their little grouping, one hand at her waist guiding her into the shade of the plant, under cover.

"Not yet. Grif is closest. Steve is with him. Mag was the farthest away." She noticed Matt didn't apologize for calling in the cavalry.

"ETA?" Slade insisted on clarification, his voice professional and concise.

Matt responded to the tone, even if he didn't quite recognize it. Kate saw the way his spine straightened. Whether he realized it or not, he was responding to the voice of command.

"Twenty minutes," Robert answered, giving Slade a narrow-eyed look.

The older brother realized what had just happened, though he didn't seem to be questioning Slade's right to take charge. Kate realized belatedly, that she'd just seen three Alphas sort out the pecking order, so to speak, with a modest amount of words and the subtlety of tone and body language. Maybe she'd learn how to read these mysterious cats after all.

"Did you two do any recon?" Slade asked, his tone clearly expecting affirmative answers.

Robert smiled, as did Matt. Of course they'd prowled around that house. They were cats, weren't they? But Kate worried for them. They were ill equipped to sense the true danger of those premises. She felt the evil and had to suppress her shivers. This wasn't your garden variety dabbler in the black arts.

No, to radiate that kind of dark energy, whoever lived there had to have been steeped in evil for decades. Maybe centuries, depending on what kind of creature they were.

This was the place. She recognized the evil taint.

Kate concentrated on the house, trying to read what she could of the miasma of red and black that swirled around it. She tuned the men and their conversation about perimeters and security systems out of her mind while she did her own sort of reconnaissance. Recon of the magical kind.

She sank into her study, watching the patterns emanating from the house and grounds. There was a definite rhythm to the dark power thrumming through the ground over there. A magical kind of security system of shields and traps. Very sophisticated. But she could nullify or work her way around most of it. There were just a few tricky spots...

She became aware of Slade touching her shoulder. She blinked and realized the two cougars were gone.

"Where did they go?" She asked the thing that popped into her mind.

"I gave them sentry duty. They're watching for their brothers. I'm sure they have every intention of storming the place in force once their older brothers get here, but we're going to outmaneuver them." His devilish smile invited her to join in his dangerous mood.

"In twenty minutes?" She looked back at the house. "It will be close, but I think we can do it."

"What did you see?" Slade immediately got down to business and she explained her thoughts and pointed out various features in the landscaping.

She was able to illuminate some of the magic so he could see it, without triggering the magical alarms that would alert their prey. She pointed out two areas that would be particularly tricky and watched Slade study them. She liked the way he deliberated and thought through his actions before proceeding. So far, she'd only known shifters who were more or less hotheads — rushing in without sparing a thought for strategy. Slade's more thoughtful approach made her feel safer both for herself and for him.

"All right. Stay here. I think I can do this on my own." Slade moved to leave her, but she grabbed his arm.

"I don't think so. What are you going to do when you find them? There's a buildup of energy in that house. Whoever is inside is up to something and it's happening as we speak. Strong as you are, I don't think you should try to handle it alone. I need to go with you. You need more magic than you have on your own."

Slade seemed to think about it, then gave in with a frustrated sigh.

"You do exactly what I say, when I say it. Got me?" His tone was gruff but his eyes spoke of his apprehension. He was worried about her. It was touching, really.

"I got you, partner," she answered softly, warmed by his concern.

They made their way with cautious steps through the magical minefield of the side yard, approaching from the neighbor's overgrown property. There were lots of bushy things that were casting long shadows as the sun sank, leaving the world painted in orange, red and purple. And shadows. Lots and lots of shadows.

Slade showed her how to slink from one shadow to the next, blending with them. She'd never be as good at stealth as he was, but with his patient guidance, she was a lot better than she would have expected.

They had to stop several times while she defused magical traps. She was able to call on the powerful earth energy that lay, unsettled, far beneath the ground. It didn't like the darkness that spread like a stain over its surface from the house. It readily rose to her lightest touch and smothered the nasty surprises the dark mage who lived within had left for the unwary.

And the benefit of having the earth on their side was that it was vastly more powerful than either of them. It could also nullify the darkness, absorbing it and dispersing it, without anyone the wiser. Those inside the house wouldn't know their traps had been destroyed until it was too late.

The telltales on the darkly pulsing shields that surrounded the place were another matter. Kate had to deal with them using her own personal energy, and it was draining. She handled the first set, but there were others. Stronger ones, the closer they drew to the house.

She was breathing hard by the time they'd gone through three sets and there were still three more to go. She felt panic rise inside her chest.

"You okay?" Slade bent close to whisper in her ear as they crouched in the shadows behind a palm.

"The shields," she panted. "They take a lot out of me."

"Aw, kitten," Slade touched her cheek, their eyes meeting. "Why didn't you say so?"

He bent his lips to hers and kissed her lightly. The kiss brought with it a flood of power, flowing from him into her, magical energy freely given and so desperately needed. He hadn't had to kiss her to accomplish the transfer of power, but she didn't mind. She liked the way he kissed and she wanted to experience more—as soon as they dealt with whoever was inside that house.

He drew back and she had to stop herself from following, begging for more of his touch, his taste, his power. She felt full of life and raring to go once more. She looked him over, searching to see if he had suffered for giving her so much energy, but he looked fine. Shifters had vast stores of magic within them, she knew, though she'd never been the recipient of an infusion of their wild energy before.

For that matter, she didn't think most shifters would be able to do what Slade had just done. He was so much more intensely magical than any of the other shifters she'd known. He had skills and abilities that the other *were* didn't even seem to be aware of. He was a mystery... and a paradox... and one of the sexiest men she'd ever known.

"Better?" His grin was temptation itself. Even in the midst of the most dangerous thing she'd ever done, he had the ability to blow her mind.

"Much. Thanks. We can go now." She had to get her mind back on their task. Slade was just too distracting.

"Not yet," he cautioned, holding her arm when she would have moved away. "I want the sun down past the peak of the roof for the next part. It'll only take a minute."

Kate was very conscious of time ticking away. They'd used up almost ten minutes already and she didn't trust the cougars not to come barreling in without checking where Slade and Kate were first. They could really mess things up and get someone hurt—or killed—if they didn't approach with more caution than she thought they were capable of right now.

"You're doing really well for a human," Slade observed, drawing her attention away from her worrying thoughts.

"Thanks," she answered, pleased down to her toes at his compliment. "To be honest, I always sort of dreamed that at least one of my birth parents was something Other, but they both died when I was a baby and I grew up in foster care, so I guess I'll never know."

Darnit. She was babbling. And this was not the time, nor the place, to be yapping about her sorry origins. What was it about this man that made her want to tell him everything, no matter how personal or embarrassing? He was definitely dangerous to her peace of mind.

"If I was a betting man, I'd say you were part siren, luring men to their happy deaths."

"Oh, that's nice," she scoffed, careful to keep her voice low so they wouldn't be heard over the natural sounds of the desert.

"I can definitely see you as the helpless seductress of the ocean. It isn't your fault if sailors toss themselves into the waves and drown trying to get to you. At least they die happy."

His teasing was sort of a backhanded compliment, so she went along with it. Was he flirting with her? It felt like flirting. And what kind of daredevil took time to flirt with a girl in the middle of a life-or-death mission?

Suddenly, she realized what this was all about. He was trying to get her mind off what they were about to do. He was distracting her. Helping her cope.

Damn. His gentle care of her only made her more attracted to him. He was such a special guy.

"Thanks," she whispered. "I know what you're trying to do and it worked. I'll be okay now. I'm recharged, thanks to you, and calmer."

"Am I that transparent?" One corner of his mouth lifted in a smile that warmed her heart.

"About as clear as mud, and you know it. But thanks for taking a minute for me to regroup. I'm good to go now."

"Ooh-rah. That's my girl." His tone was approving and he stroked her hair once before turning to continue their treacherous path. She followed along, a little more in love with him than she'd already been.

Love? Oh, man.

Yeah, if she was being honest with herself, she had to admit, she had it bad for the mysterious cat shifter. He fulfilled all her wildest fantasies about what a man could be and then some. Everything she'd seen about him attracted her on every level.

She was in serious danger of losing her heart to him forever. When he left—not *if* he left, because his time here had a definite, and short, time span—she could be destroyed. But she'd be damned if she saw any way out of it. Slade was just too attractive for his own good and she was powerless to resist him.

And they had a job to do. As the fourth set of shields confronted her, she set to work with renewed energy, knowing he'd be there for her if she needed to recharge again. They made a good team and she'd never forget this night, or the man at her side—if she lived through the confrontation to come, that is.

CHAPTER FIVE

The fifth and sixth set of shields went down even easier than the first few had. Now that Slade knew how to help her by feeding her energy, they were working more in tandem and were more powerful than either had been alone. The effect of shared energy was even greater than he'd been led to believe.

Or maybe it was just the fact that he was sharing energy with Kate. Maybe there was something special about her that affected his power so strongly. He wouldn't be surprised. The woman herself affected him as no woman ever had. He wanted so badly to be inside her, to know whether she was silent, or a screamer, when he made love to her. He wanted to hold her in the aftermath and bask in the knowledge that he had brought her pleasure.

He wanted a lot of things he'd never contemplated before, and didn't know if he deserved. He was only here for a short time. A mission that would be over sooner rather than later. Did he dare get involved with a woman who could break his seldom-seen heart?

Kate frightened him. *Him.* The big, bad, black cat. His mother would laugh if she knew he was afraid of a small, *human* woman. But it was the feelings she aroused in him that scared him most. Protectiveness was something he'd felt all his life, but the possessiveness and need to claim one particular woman, was new and scary.

Better to concentrate on their mission. They were close to the house now and he felt the evil building. Kate was right. Whoever was in there was up to something big, and bad, and magical in the extreme.

Slade gave a passing thought to the backup he could have called. The Spec Ops boys would have been of little help in this situation, though. Most of them had no magic sense at all. They were good ground forces. Superior at stealth. But when it came down to it, this was a magical fight.

Calling in the cavalry tonight would have been like bringing a knife to a gunfight. Slade was almost glad there had been no time to consider it. Matt's discovery and the subsequent time squeeze made it impossible to get those guys here, and they wouldn't have been of much help anyway. No, this was a job for Slade's specialized abilities. His and Kate's—much as he hated putting her in any sort of danger.

He'd do what he could to keep her safe, but he needed her talents, and her help, to get through this magical minefield of a property. They'd made it through the yard, but the house would probably be even worse.

There was a window about two meters to their right. He'd try to see what he could through it before they went any farther. Motioning to Kate to stay put in the shadow of the foundation, Slade crept up to the glass and peered in as stealthily as he could.

The room was empty. Nobody saw him from the inside, but he could see through the open door of the empty room into the hall. From there, he could see into another area that looked like the great room of the McMansion. A man was seated on the floor of that room with his back to the window Slade looked through.

Slade sent all of his senses out, seeking. He breathed deep and recognized the scent of the male from the crime scene, but the female scent was missing. In fact, there was no other scent than the male's, and no other heartbeat. In the desert night, he could only hear Kate, himself, the man in the house and the two cougars still manning the perimeter like good little kitties.

The rest of the house was empty. He'd bet his life on it. Which left them with the single opponent he'd seen through the window.

Slade motioned to Kate, beckoning her closer. He pointed, indicating that she should take a quick look. Her head popped up and then down again, her eyes wide.

She stepped right up to Slade and spoke near his ear. He liked the feel of her warm body against his, but there wasn't time to explore the feelings she roused in him. They had work to do and he had to keep his mind on business, dammit.

"He's facing east," she said. "Preparing a ritual. Looks like he is inside a scribed circle. I think they turned the great room into a ritual space. If he's inside that circle, he'll be harder to reach," she added, confirming his thoughts.

He'd picked up a thing or two about human magic rites in his life, but not enough to claim to be any sort of expert. Which is where Kate came in. She knew a lot more about human ways than he did. Most of his magic was instinctual, and animal in nature.

"So we need to draw him out." Easier said than done, he feared.

"Ideally," she confirmed. "But how?"

"Follow me." A plan was forming even as he moved through the yard toward the front of the house.

"What are you going to do?" Kate was doing her best to keep up with his fast pace, but he couldn't slow down. Time was running out before the cougars showed up in force.

"Stay here and keep watch," he said as they reached the corner of the house. "I'm going to draw him out."

"How?"

He spared her a smile. "I'm going to ring the doorbell."

She grabbed his arm. "You can't! He'll realize what you are the minute he opens the door."

"Calm down, kitten. He's never seen me before. I only got here this morning. Watch and learn." And with that, he used a skill he alone possessed—as far as he knew.

"Bright Lady," she gasped, and he knew his little trick was working.

From one breath to the next, Slade's strong magical aura just winked out of existence.

"How'd you do that?" She was shocked by his ability to mask his true nature.

Kate had never seen, or even heard of such a thing before. If she'd met him now for the first time, she'd think he was purely human. Not a glimmer of power escaped whatever he'd done to hide it.

"Stay put. You'll know when it's time to act," was all he said before he walked away, heading straight for the front door of the big house.

She couldn't believe his audacity as he rang the bell and waited.

A moment later the front door opened and the man was there, looking annoyed. Slade didn't say a word, but reached out, trying to grab the guy, and that's when all hell broke loose. The mage wasn't going to come quietly.

He shoved at the air between himself and Slade, using his magical energy to send Slade several yards away, fighting all the way. This was it. Slade had told her she'd recognize the moment to act and this was definitely it.

Kate summoned her will and the potent and endless magic of the earth, and pulled at the mage, drawing him out of the doorway and down the steps, using his own momentum against him. She drew him right into Slade's reach.

While the mage's attention was split between them, Slade took full advantage and grabbed the man in a choke hold. The mage struggled, but he was a small guy, not very physical, and Kate kept the magical attack on him so he couldn't do much more than try to respond — and that not very successfully.

"Can you do that thing you did before?" Slade asked, keeping hold of his prisoner, though the mage was gaining strength as the initial shock of the attack wore off.

She knew what he meant. Slade wanted her to drain the mage of all his power, as she'd done to Wayne.

Kate hadn't done it since Wayne, and she hesitated to strike out at the mage, lest she hit Slade too, but she knew the Goddess she served would help her, if she asked. The Lady would surely know good from evil and only purge the evil one, not the very good man that was holding him. Right? She had to trust that it would be so... as Slade apparently did.

He nodded to her, holding her gaze, imparting a bit of his courage to her. She nodded back, willing to try.

Tapping into Mother Earth's endless fire and saying a silent prayer for Her divine guidance, Kate spoke the ancient words she'd been taught after that first night in the stone circle so many years before. She called on the earth to cleanse the evil from the man and purify his spirit, leaving behind only what power had been good.

That didn't leave much. The mage had lots of bad energy to purge and it took long minutes of intense concentration on Kate's part to do the deed. All the while, the mage writhed in agony as the Lady's purifying Light poured through him.

It didn't stay. It couldn't stay inside a heart that held such hatred. It merely passed through, taking all his magical power with it.

By the time she was done, the mage was a mage no more.

Slade felt the full effect of Kate's power and was awed by it. She was truly the hand of the Goddess, as the Lady's purifying Light poured through the man who struggled against Slade's hold. The power touched Slade too, but didn't burn. Instead, he felt the welcoming goodness of the Lady's Light like a balm to his soul.

It was the most amazing feeling. And Kate—little, *human* Kate—wielded this power. Slade looked at her with renewed respect.

The man writhed in his arms, screaming as the power of the Lady's Light cleansed him. He struggled at first and Slade held him so he couldn't attack Kate. The hold became one more of support than restraint as the magic drained away until it was no more.

Slade actually felt it leave and be swallowed up by the earth beneath his feet. The pulsing negativity of the area went with it and the whole place began to glow with power while the Lady's Light cleansed the earth, dispersing the evil for all time.

The man slumped in his hold, sliding to the ground. He was empty. No magic. Very little life energy left. He'd tied up too much of his own essence in the evil he worked. Blood magic did that.

Slade heard running feet and he turned his head to find the entire compliment of Redstone brothers pounding up the path. They were quiet enough, even in human form, that Kate didn't hear them yet, but Slade certainly did.

He pulled the man to his feet and shoved him toward the cougars.

"Don't kill him yet. He's harmless for now," Slade said, knowing the man was aware enough to understand when he jerked in his hold. "He's been defanged."

"Permanently," Kate added, coming closer and showing a lot more spirit than Slade had expected.

The power of the Lady was still running through her. She glowed with the Light when Slade glanced at her and he had to force himself to look away. The cougars couldn't see it, but they probably felt something when they paused in their headlong rush to take charge of the man that had taken part in the murder of their mother.

"What did you do to him?" Grif asked, taking the lead, as was his right as Alpha. He looked at Kate with caution in his expression, as if he'd only just realized the priestess had real power of her own to call on.

"Purged all his evil," she answered. "Unless he embraces the Light, he will never work magic again."

"You can do that?" Steve asked. The cougars spread out in a semi-circle around them.

"Yep," she answered, smacking her lips. Saucy. She was enjoying the surprise on the cougars' faces.

Especially Steve's. She had always thought him the most attractive of the brothers. Tall, rugged, capable and handsome in a manly way.

Kate had once had a thing for him, though it would never have worked out. In all likelihood, he didn't see her as anything other than some frail human priestess, always in need of protecting from the big, bad shifters. He had treated her like fragile porcelain—when he bothered to acknowledge her existence at all.

She had always been attracted to the strong, silent types. Steve was that, in spades. So was Slade—though he was on a whole other level than mild-mannered, mostly-silent Steve.

Slade, now... He was something even more deadly to her soft heart and unruly attraction. He lit her up like a barn on fire and there was precious little she could do to stop her incendiary attraction to the mysterious man.

"She's done it before," Slade backed up her claim. "It's permanent, painful and has no chance of recovery unless he turns from his evil path."

The prisoner gulped. It wasn't much of a noise, but it was definitely audible to shifter ears.

The cougars switched their attention as one, from Kate and Slade, to their captive.

"You murdered my mother, you spineless bastard," Grif advanced on the cringing man. Slade was a solid barrier at his back. The toad wasn't going anywhere.

Slade would rather have done this elsewhere, but it would be best to take advantage of the shock of the past few minutes. Kick the bastard while he was down. Don't give him a chance to regroup and start thinking. Question him now and see what he spilled.

Slade scanned the area around the house and realized they were well hidden from the road. The vegetation was overgrown—probably on purpose in this guy's case—and acted as a shield to prying eyes.

The front door had an extended entry way that was like a little porch with two big, white columns on either side. Slade backed the man up to one of the columns, pulling his arms behind him, around the fluted white pole. He pulled a plastic zip tie from his pocket—something he'd put in there even before he left

Montana, knowing he was going on a mission where he might need restraints—and secured the guy's hands behind the pole.

He wouldn't leave him there long. Only while they had the advantage of his shock to work with. They couldn't stay here too long anyway. He might have backup that would come to see what happened. Slade wanted Kate long gone and the cougars well hidden long before anything like that happened. But they had an opportunity to exploit the prisoner's imbalance right now and Slade had been playing this game long enough to know when to take advantage of a situation like this.

"What do you say to that?" Grif went on. "What do you say to the sons of the woman you killed?" Grif's voice got deeper and scarier rather than louder, which served them well in this case.

"I didn't kill her," the man whined. "She did it. She wanted her pelt. Not me. I only got the leftovers. And now it's gone. Gone." He began to whimper and sob as he probably realized all his power was gone, never to return.

Slade was almost glad to see him suffer after what he'd done, but another part of him felt sorrow for everyone who had lost so much in this terrible situation. The man's actions had brought about his own downfall and so much pain for so many people. Such was the way of evil. Preventing it from running rampant through the world was Slade's *raison d'etre*. Had been ever since he'd grown up and grown weary of the senselessness of war for war's sake.

The only battles Slade engaged in now were against evil. He'd been very careful since his early days in the business to pick his opponents with great care. There had been many in the world who qualified as evil in his book. He'd fought them all at one time or another, but since retiring from active duty and specializing for the Company—and the Lords—he'd been even more selective.

This was a justified takedown, even though everything about this situation left a bad feeling in his soul. It also left a pain in his heart for the innocent woman who'd been this toad's victim. The former mage had wanted the matriarch's power and he'd taken it by taking her blood. That could not stand. That kind of evil could not be allowed to exist. Not on Slade's watch.

"Who is she? Who is your partner?" Kate asked in a quiet, powerful voice, drawing Slade's attention away from his dark thoughts.

"She'll kill me." Terror showed in his wild eyes.

"You're already dead to her," Slade said quietly. "You have no magic. Never will again. She won't want you. You're no good to her now."

The prisoner sobbed again.

"I'll tell you what. You tell us what we want to know and we'll take you away from here where she can't find you," Slade whispered.

"You're going to kill me," the man objected.

"Maybe. Maybe not. Right now, you've got information we want. You play nice with us, we might let you go. Too much trouble to hide a body in this day and age." Slade inspected his fingernails, trying to convey how little it meant to him. "And you're no danger to anyone anymore. You've got no power and no way to get it back. You're Goddess touched, my man. Your old friends will smite you on sight."

The man began to cry in earnest. Pathetic. He was going to crumble like a cookie in a two-year-old's fist at any moment.

"I'm sorry," he cried. "I'm so sorry."

Slade looked over at Kate, surprised to his core. Could the Lady's power have had that much of an effect on this guy so quickly? Kate smiled. She knew something. Maybe she'd seen this kind of reaction before with Wayne. She held his gaze and nodded, and he had his answer. She'd been expecting this kind of change.

Amazing what the Goddess could do when She put her mind to it.

"Sorry?" Robert tried to stalk forward but Grif held out his hand, motioning him to stillness. All the brothers watched the prisoner warily, clearly confused.

"Are you going to come quietly? I'll be honest with you," Slade said to the man, who had quieted. "We're your best option at the moment. And frankly, we're not going to give you any choice. You either come with us voluntarily — which will be easier for you — or we take you anyway, and probably bang you around a bit, just for kicks."

The prisoner seemed to think a moment, then sag in defeat. "I'll come quietly," he said finally. "You're right. I'm already dead if they find me like this."

"Good," Slade said approvingly, cutting the zip tie with a partially shifted claw.

He nodded to the younger brothers, refastening the man's hands with another zip tie now that he was free of the column. Matt, Robert and Steve moved closer at

Grif's nod to take custody of the man, but he turned to Kate, suddenly tense.

"Take the chalice. Don't let her get it. She needs it for her crazy plan. It's in the circle."

Kate nodded, seeming to understand. "When is she coming? When is she planning to do her ceremony?"

"Tomorrow night. At the new moon," he replied. "Take the chalice and hide it. She won't be able to do what she wants without it." The man's terror was fading and with it, his consciousness.

He seemed open now, telling them things without being prodded, but his strength was failing. Even as the cougars moved close to him, he collapsed, passing out at their feet. They let him fall and he landed hard. Slade didn't really blame them. He had helped murder their mother, after all. Forgiveness — if it ever came — would be a long time coming.

"Pick him up and put him in the truck," Grif ordered his brothers and they followed his instructions none too gently. "Guard him. We'll be down shortly."

That left Slade and Kate with Grif and Mag, the quiet brother who came somewhere in the middle of the brood of siblings. Slade hadn't gotten a good read on him, but he seemed as steady and strong as the rest of the Redstone brothers.

"I have to go into the house," Kate said, taking the bull by the horns even before the prisoner was out of sight.

"Is it safe?" Grif asked, concern on his face.

"No," Slade answered, scowling. He didn't want her going in there, but he knew they had to at least look into what the prisoner had said.

"We can do it," Kate said, meeting his gaze and smiling gently. "Together. Like we did before."

Oh, he liked that. Something inside him purred happily at the way she paired them up as a team. The cat liked having a partner in crime that had already proven their skills and courage. The cat inside him liked *her*.

It was the man who worried for her safety. He wanted to protect her. Keep her safe. Keep her to himself.

Hmm. He would have to think about these strange, new impulses she brought out in him. Later. They didn't have time for self-examination right now.

No, now was the time for action.

"Okay," he gave in, gratified by her smile. "We do this together." He glanced back at the cougars. "You two will have to act as rearguard this time and wait for the all clear. You can't see the magic the way we can, and this place was booby trapped in ways I've never encountered before. It was hard enough getting across his yard. I can only imagine what he's got inside."

"Understood," Grif nodded, clearly unhappy with having to take a supporting role, but willing to allow the experts in magic to do their thing.

"There was a shield here," Kate observed quietly as they approached the front door. "It's gone but I still can feel traces of it."

"It was probably blown when you called down the Light. Not much could stand in the face of that." Slade knew there was admiration in his tone. Hell, he was damned impressed by what she had done and he wouldn't soon forget how powerful she was when her skills were pressed into service. "There might be something like a blast radius at work here. The farther we get from the front porch, the weaker the effect. Keep an eye out."

"Yeah." She walked a few steps into the house and stopped, looking around carefully. "I think you're probably right. There are shields on every doorway and arch. Some of the closer ones are flickering. You see that?"

Slade looked where she pointed. Oh, yeah. Dark power swirled like a fog but the openings closer to the front door were definitely damaged. Weakened. They would come down easily.

Not so the archway that led into the great room. While somewhat damaged, the shielding there had probably been thicker to begin with. There was a violent swirl of red, brown and black. A cloudy miasma that made Slade seethe just looking at it.

It was evil. Blood magic.

"We need to get into the great room," he reminded her unnecessarily. "Through that." He pointed to the swirling cloud of dark magic.

Kate took a deep breath at his side and squared her shoulders. "We can do it," she whispered, almost to herself.

She had courage, he'd give her that. Most human women he had known—if they could have seen something like what faced them now—would have run away, screaming in terror. Not Kate. She was cautious, of course. She wasn't a fool. But she had a strength of character, a toughness of spirit, Slade had seldom found in any female who was not also a shifter.

Without warning, Kate made a sign of protection in the air in front of her. Slade felt, as well as saw, the bright spark of protection as a shield of Light surrounded them both like transparent armor.

"I think we'd better take some precautions, don't you?" Kate smiled over at him. "Just in case."

"Good thinking." Slade liked that she'd spun her shield to protect them both, but he was concerned about how much energy it would take out of her. Even with him feeding her power, eventually they would both be too weak to keep up the protection. They had to work quickly, but safely.

"The cougars can always pull us out if we collapse," she joked, somehow reading his mind. "I figured we were close to the end of our usefulness here — and very close to something potentially more dangerous than anything we've faced to this point — so the extra expenditure of magical energy is justified in my mind."

He thought about her words for a moment, agreeing with her logic.

"Let's get in, get the chalice and get out as quickly as possible."

"Agreed." Kate turned her head, focusing on the dark archway that led to the great room. "I don't see anything from here to the arch," she observed as she moved one step forward, advancing slowly into the foyer. "I think the Light destroyed whatever was here, closest to the front porch."

"I don't sense anything either," Slade told her, moving with her, step by cautious step.

They made it to within five feet of the arch safely. As they had surmised, the action on the porch had nullified anything within the blast radius, as Slade had put it, but that archway was definitely up and running, with all its evil intent intact.

Slade knew a few different ways to counteract such things. Of course, adding Kate's magic into the mix allowed for new and better possibilities. The shield she had put around them, for example, was not something Slade had ever seen before.

"Can we project out from behind your shield?" he asked. "Or do you have to drop it to work?"

"We can send energy out but it should slow or stop anything coming back at us."

"Neat trick." His respect for her abilities was increasing beyond the high point it had already reached. She continued to impress him. Each time he thought he had her figured out, she'd pull another rabbit out of her hat.

One thing was for sure, being around her was never boring. He would have laughed at that thought if the circumstances weren't so dire.

"What do you propose?" She didn't turn her head, intent on studying the darkness they would have to penetrate without unleashing it on themselves or others, but he knew he had her attention.

"How about the old bait and switch?"

That made her look at him. "You mean one of us trigger it while the other acts?"

"Yeah. I'll test it out. You give it the old whammy. You up for it?" Slade was excited by the challenge and happy to have found a way to keep her back—at least a little—from the main area of action. He'd be taking on the full wrath of the magical protection while she worked from behind him.

She eyed him with mingled suspicion and worry in her beautiful eyes before nodding once in agreement. Without giving her time to change her mind, Slade stepped away from her side, expecting her protection to fade, but much to his surprise, the shield of Light stayed around him. It was even stronger than he had thought.

And there she went, surprising him again. Damn, he liked that a lot. Hells, he liked *her* a lot. Which was something he wanted to explore, in great detail, once they had a little time to themselves.

For now, they had to get through the archway and conquer whatever waited within.

Slade sent out his best countermeasure through the shield of Light, aimed at the roiling black, red and brown blood magic. The combination looked like dark rust—or dried blood—which was probably what powered such a foul thing.

The dark miasma reached out tendrils of its foul self at him, seeking to attack, or at the very least, trap him in its coils. The Light protected him, as did his own magical protections, but the reaction from the barrier in the archway was much stronger than he'd expected.

"Now, Kate!" Slade called out as the barrier reached for him again, stronger this time.

He concentrated his power and struck back, knocking it down somewhat, but his magic alone wasn't going to be enough. Then Kate joined in.

A blast of pure white Light broke through the roiling cloud, making it bleed energy into the floor, then through it, to whatever lay beneath, and ultimately into the earth. Kate's power shored up

Slade's and together they were able to wipe the archway of all taint, banishing it and dispersing it.

Kate let up the onslaught at the same time Slade released his own attack. The barrier was well and truly gone.

Slade took a deep breath and turned to survey his partner, his senses alert to any and all threats. So far, nothing took offense at the destruction of the barrier. Good.

Kate seemed to wilt, but her spirit was high. They'd both expended a great deal more energy than Slade had expected. He took an involuntary step toward her.

"Are you okay?"

Kate nodded, biting her lip for a moment as she caught her breath. "Good to go," she replied, somewhat unconvincingly, but the smile and thumbs up that accompanied her white lie made him feel both pride and joy in her indomitable spirit.

Slade spared a minute to let the two Redstones know that the foyer was safe if they needed to advance into the house. Grif and Mag nodded, but the older brother looked pointedly at his watch and Slade knew they were running low on time. He turned back to Kate with renewed determination.

"Stay behind me, kitten," he instructed softly.

"No problem. I'm not too proud to admit, I need a few seconds to regroup mentally, if not physically. That cloud was really disgusting. Slimy." She shivered.

"Evil," he agreed. "Sometimes it manifests like that." Slade shrugged.

"You've seen this before?"

He found it oddly satisfying to have surprised her for a change.

"A few times, but not exactly in this configuration. This whole house is a new one on me."

"Me too," she agreed, moving closer to him as they prepared to enter the great room.

CHAPTER SIX

As Kate entered the great room, the awful sight that met her eyes took breath away.

"Sweet merciful Mother of All," she whispered as her attention was drawn by the pulsing power of the dark circle that had been permanently inscribed in the hard wood floor. That barrier would not be easy to cross.

Beyond it — in fact, all around the perimeter of the large room — were cages. Cages that held occupants of varying sizes and shapes. Many of them were cats. Several started mewling pitifully as she walked in, just behind Slade.

"None of these animals are shifters, thank the Goddess," Slade said quickly, his nose pointedly sniffing the air.

"But they are magical. I think they're familiars," Kate said, walking to the closest cage and peering inside at the weak, fluffy, black and white cat that lay so forlornly within. "Valerie can help with this. She's got a special affinity for these kinds of creatures."

"Kate," Slade's tone caught her attention. "Something's moving inside the circle. Behind the altar."

Kate looked at the circle once more, realizing the small, low table, which was about the size of a small ottoman or large footstool, was what Slade accurately described as an altar. She remembered when they looked in the window, that the mage had been sitting on the floor inside the circle, facing the altar, doing something. She dreaded what she might see. For all they knew, he could have been calling demons when they interrupted him.

"The good news is, I think the perimeter of the room is clear. The simple magic of these familiars apparently foiled whatever attempts our guy made to work his evil outside the circle," she said quickly. "I think we can move around the room freely. Whatever's inside the circle won't be able to get out until we break it, and the familiars' energies have kept the rest of the room clear."

"Good." Slade looked around as if confirming her ideas for himself. "Stay here. I'm going to go around and see what's lurking on the other side of the altar."

She nodded, but he was already off, stalking silently around the room. As he went, the familiars who had the strength, rose in their cages to watch him. Many sets of feline eyes followed his progress with clear curiosity.

He cursed under his breath as he saw whatever it was that crouched behind the small altar.

"It's a bear cub, and it's bleeding," he announced quietly. "I think the bastard was trying to fill the chalice with this little one's blood. There's a very ornate goblet lying on its side next to the poor thing and blood all over the floor back here."

"We have to help it," Kate said without hesitation.

"Yeah," Slade answered, a pained expression on his face. "But first we have to get to the cub and then we have to subdue it. The little one may be weak, but it is also scared witless. And I can't smell it or hear it. The circle must be containing everything from within. I can't scent whether it's a shifter or just a baby bear. We also can't hear it and it can't hear us. It can see me though, and it's getting angry."

"Then we'd better figure out how to get to it and get the chalice."

"And get the hells out of here," Slade agreed. "Any ideas?"

"Yeah, one."

Kate reached into her pocket and took out the small bag of herbs and stones she usually kept with her. They were part of her magical stock and trade, and she'd come to learn over recent years, that she never quite knew when she'd be called upon to work different kinds of magic.

Kate walked around the circle, placing small, semi-precious stones at the four cardinal points hoping to contain whatever would be unleashed when she broke the perimeter of the evil circle. If the bear was more than just a bear, she didn't want it running amok before they could stop it.

To that end, Kate set up her own barrier of protection around the evil one, encasing it as best she could under the circumstances. She did it quickly and with as little fuss as possible, regaining her strength and centering herself as she went. She got a good look at the bleeding bear cub. It looked so innocent, but without certain knowledge of what it really was, Kate was still suspicious. Too often in her experience, evil masqueraded as something innocent.

The bear watched her with equal suspicion from its position on the floor when she walked around that side of the circle. There was intelligence behind those soft brown eyes and Kate worried anew about what sort of creature they might be dealing with.

There was only one way to find out.

Kate raised her arms as she raised the dome of protection outside the circle, enfolding it in the power of the Light of the Lady which showed in faint sparks to her mage sight. Kate knew Slade saw it too. He looked at it with approval before turning back to her.

"Handy," he commented with a slight grin. "Now what?"

"One of us has to break the outer line of the circle." She grimaced as she thought of what could happen after they took that final, irrevocable step.

"What do you recommend?" Slade looked to her for advice, which she found both frightening and gratifying. She didn't want to advise him—or anyone, for that matter—to take an action that might result in their injury, or even their death.

"A bit of salt should do it," she answered softly.

"That's all?" Slade looked surprised.

"Sometimes simple is better. I always keep a little salt in my pouch. It's more powerful than most people know." She lifted the little bag in her hands. "This salt was consecrated in the circle of stones at the full moon, under the Lady's guidance, but even regular table salt usually works. This stuff just has that little extra whammy." She opened the small pouch that held the salt. It was a mix of fine and more granular crystals and it was pink.

She realized immediately that Slade understood the significance of the color.

"That's Himalayan." He paused beside her, looking down at the pink crystals in her hand. "I think that means this is my task, don't you?" He reached out to take the salt from her, but she stopped him, clasping his arm and looking up into his eyes.

"I'm worried, Slade. That bear might be something else entirely. Once we break the barrier, I have no idea what will happen. It could be bad. Very bad." She tried her best to caution him. Something inside—some inner sense that she would never fully understand—made her fear for him.

She couldn't lose him now. She had only just found him.

"You hold the barrier. I'll deal with whatever is inside. Don't worry. I've done this kind of thing before." He reached down to kiss her lips sweetly while taking the little pouch of salt from her trembling hands.

And then he was gone. Moving away, toward the evil circle.

"Just pour the salt over the line, breaking it," she coached, all but gnashing her teeth with worry.

And she had a right to be worried. The moment Slade poured out the pink salt from the pouch and it touched the dark line on the floor, things happened in super fast slow motion.

The bear roared, no longer a bear as it changed and shifted into a much larger, deadlier form. It leapt for Slade, claws extended. The claws became hands, but the sharp nails remained, raking over Slade's body, slicing through his clothing as if it were nothing.

"Miranda, no!" Mag's shout came from the archway behind Kate. The younger Redstone had entered without her realizing it and he seemed to recognize the creature inside the circle whose glistening fangs were even now bearing down on Slade's unprotected neck.

It was a woman.

It was a vampire. And she was crazed from starvation and blood loss.

Dear Goddess, no!

"Miranda!" Mag dashed into the room, stopping only feet from the woman who held Slade immobile, bleeding from a multitude of cuts she had inflicted in less than a few seconds.

She seemed to pause, her fangs a breath away from Slade's skin, and look at Mag Redstone.

Her red-rimmed, wild eyes cleared and she stopped, dropping the bone-crushing hold she'd had on Slade. He slumped away from her as she moved toward the younger Redstone.

"Careful, Mag!" Grif spoke in a low growl, just entering the room.

"It's okay. This is Miranda. She's a friend of mine. Sweetheart, what have they done to you?" Mag's voice broke as he held out his arms and the blood-stained vampiress walked into his embrace as if finding an oasis in the desert.

"Magnus?" Her voice was confused, weak, but still held that vampire mojo Kate had heard about. She could enslave every man in the room just by saying *come hither*, but she wasn't doing it on purpose. It was part of her magic that she had to consciously tamp down.

It was clear the woman was beyond doing that at the moment. She was weak and injured. Still bleeding and more than a little out of it.

"I'm here, sweetheart. I've got you." Mag took her in his arms, crooning to her gently, clearly familiar with the woman and willing to put himself at risk for her sake. She could still go crazy and rip his throat out in her hunger—and it was clear to Kate she had been deprived of the blood that fueled her existence for a long time.

"She needs to feed," Kate whispered.

"I know." Mag Redstone met her gaze over the vampire's matted blond hair. He guided her lips deliberately to his throat and closed his eyes in obvious pleasure as she nuzzled him. She bit into his skin almost delicately, as if she cared for him and didn't want to hurt him.

Judging by the expression on Mag's face, hurt was the farthest thing from what he was feeling at the moment. Kate looked away, turning to Slade. He watched the vampire and Mag for a moment before turning his gaze to meet Kate's.

"It's probably safe inside here for you now, except for that." Slade pointed as he spoke in a pained voice. She followed his gesture to see the chalice on the floor, still bleeding its red burden into the hardwood.

"That's what we came for." She walked toward him carefully. She didn't like being inside the zone that had once been so disgustingly evil. "This place is going to need a thorough cleansing before it'll be completely safe for even non-magical folk," she observed with distaste as the oily feel of the circle rubbed up against her skin. "Are you okay?"

Slade didn't look okay. She bit her lip, worrying. He didn't seem to be bleeding badly, though the slices the vampire had made with her sharp claws didn't look comfortable.

"Just hurt in my pride is all." Slade grimaced as he tried to get up.

Kate reached to help him and realized he was weaker than he looked. Her eyes narrowed as she gazed at him.

"You sure?"

He shook his head just once and mouthed the words, *not here.* She got the message, but she didn't like it. Not one bit. Still, she'd go along with his wishes as long as she didn't think it would hurt him more.

"Let's grab the chalice and go," Slade said through clenched lips. He was facing away from the cougars, though Grif was scowling at his younger brother, who was still caught in the surprisingly gentle grip of the vampire.

"I don't want to touch it," she admitted, contemplating the chalice on the floor in front of them.

"Don't you dare," Slade chastised her, showing renewed spirit. "I'd give you my shirt to wrap it in, but it's sliced to ribbons and wouldn't be very effective. You need something made of natural fabric. Wool or cotton. Even leather. No synthetics," he instructed as she looked around. There wasn't much in the room and what little fabric there was didn't fit the bill.

"I've got an idea."

Kate emptied the contents of her small, cloth bag, stuffing the items into every pocket she had available. It wasn't comfortable, but it would work. The bag was small, but it would fit the chalice. The blood would probably ruin her nice little bag, but that couldn't be helped. This was too important to worry about a bag that could easily be replaced.

She opened the now-empty bag over the chalice and used the fabric to shield her fingers as she grabbed the rim of the metal goblet, trying to upend it to empty the rest of the blood out of it before she maneuvered it into her bag. It took a few moments, but her plan worked like a charm. The chalice just fit into the bag, with enough room to close it securely. The ceremonial object had been contained for the moment. They would deal with dispersing its evil power — if that could be done — once they were someplace safe.

Kate secured the bag over her shoulder and then turned to help Slade, but he waved her away.

"Take down your circle and free the animals. I was able to scent *them*." *Unlike the vampire* went unsaid between them, but she knew what he meant. "They're no threat and we can't leave them here."

Nodding, she moved swiftly around the room, checking on each of the familiars and unlocking their cages. Once free, most were able to move under their own power. She had to carry one small kitten, but the rest followed her without question. They knew the feeling of good, Goddess-given magic when they felt it.

When she had them all free, she returned to Slade and helped him stand. He leaned on her even more than she'd expected, and her worry for him was renewed. He staggered out of the now-defunct circle on the floor and toward the archway, one arm around her shoulders and a trail of a dozen animals — mostly cats — in their wake.

The vampire had stopped nibbling on Mag, Kate was glad to see, but both wore expressions of euphoria. Mag lifted the woman in his arms and strode out of the house without so much as a by-your-leave to his concerned older brother. Grif watched him go for a moment before Kate and Slade drew even with him.

Seeing them, Grif helped Kate support Slade on the other side and they made their way quickly down to the street where a cluster of vehicles had been left.

Grif and Steve had come in one pickup truck, which was empty. Mag was already loading the groggy but smiling vampire into his sportscar. Matt and Robert were moving Robert's motorcycle into the bushes, hiding it, while Steve silently watched over the unconscious mage in a full-size SUV. That left the rented SUV Slade had driven.

"Do you need help with him?" Grif asked Kate directly, bypassing Slade, who seemed annoyed.

"No. She doesn't need help. I'm still awake here," Slade groused.

"Not for long by the looks of it," Grif replied with a grimace.

"It's okay. I can drive the SUV," Kate assured the Alpha cougar. "I'll take him back to my place. I can help him better there and I doubt there's anything else we can do tonight." She looked behind her, gratified to see the little parade of familiars that continued to follow them. The kitten had fallen asleep in her hand and was purring against her palm even as she inadvertently jostled it, helping support Slade.

"All right," Grif agreed, guiding them to the rental vehicle and inspecting it before helping settle Slade in the front passenger seat. "We're all going to be at the homestead except Steve, who I'm leaving on watch here tonight, and Mag. I'm not sure where he went with that vamp, but I won't allow her in the same house with Belinda."

"For what it's worth," Kate faced the angry Alpha. "She was being held prisoner by the mage. He was draining her blood into the chalice. From what I could see, she wasn't a willing participant. I'd advise you to listen to her story before you take any action. Plus, Mag seems to know her."

"Yeah." Grif sighed running one hand through his sandy hair. "That's what I'm worried about." He moved his gaze from the couple who were already on their way down the street in Mag's sports car, to Kate. "What about the critters?" Grif looked pointedly down to his feet where no less than three housecats were twining around his legs. He seemed more amused than annoyed.

"They can come with me for now, but I think Valerie should take a look at them as soon as we get home. Can you send her to my place? I don't want to let them loose on the neighborhood until we're sure they're okay."

"I'll call ahead and tell her to be ready." Grif bent to scoop one of the injured cats up as Kate opened the back door of the SUV. The animals who were able, hopped up on their own and picked out spots on the seats or floorboards. She had to help a few of the creatures that were either ill-equipped to jump that high or too weak or injured to manage it, but it didn't take long before all of the familiars were settled comfortably. A little pulse of her magic ensured they would all remain calm for the duration of the ride, barring any unforeseen circumstances.

"We'll convoy it home, just in case," Grif said as he closed the back door behind the last animal. "We should stick together. Strength in numbers and all that. Want to take the lead? You can call my cell if you sense any bad magic ahead of us. The boys and the prisoner will be in the middle and I'll be riding rear-guard."

"Sounds like a plan." She watched Robert hand his motorcycle keys to Steve. The older brother melted away into the dark as soon as he pocketed the keys to his ride home.

Kate was worried when Slade didn't put in his thoughts. Turning back to him, she saw his eyes were closed and his head was back against the headrest. He looked paler than he had before and her concern mounted.

Grif left and checked the SUV with the prisoner before hopping into his pickup.

Kate got into the driver's seat of Slade's rented SUV and started the car one-handed before turning to check on Slade. His eyes were open and he was looking at her. Good. He hadn't passed out. She counted that as a good sign.

"Can you hold her?" Kate lifted a sleeping kitten in one hand. The little thing couldn't be more than a couple of weeks old.

"Yeah, she can sit on my lap." He reached out to secure the little ball of fluff as Kate gently placed the kitten on his thigh. Through it all, the baby cat remained sound asleep and purring.

Kate pulled away from the curb and steered the SUV back toward friendlier parts of town.

"Okay, we're alone. Tell me what's going on," she began in a no-nonsense tone. She wanted to know what was up with him and she wouldn't take no for an answer this time.

"Feels like a couple of broken ribs. That vamp packed a wallop and I'm ashamed to admit, she got the jump on me. Damn, she was strong." His words were strained as he clutched his side.

"She's a vampire. There's no shame in one of them getting the drop on you—even for a shifter of your stature." She pulled out into traffic. "They're fast and they can take any form they want if they're old and skilled enough. Her strength probably came out of desperation. She was crazed with blood loss when she attacked you. I'm sure the mage was starving her and tying her down with his dark blood magics, to keep her as docile as possible before he killed her. She'll probably be grateful that you rang the doorbell when you did. I have little doubt you saved her life."

"That's one way of looking at it," Slade mused. "Hope she sees it that way. I certainly don't want to tangle with her again anytime soon. As it is..." he paused to gasp as the SUV hit a bump Kate couldn't avoid, "...I'm going to be handicapped for a while. Dammit."

"Not if I can help it," she promised him, already planning the healing ceremony she would perform when she got him home. "Sorry about the bumps. This road isn't the greatest, and I'm trying to avoid as many potholes as I can."

"It's all right."

She took his comment on several different levels. They were all right after everything they'd been through that night. That meant something. And she was sure she could make him really *all right* after a little healing magic and maybe a good night's sleep.

Yeah, they'd be okay.

One bad guy down. One to go.

CHAPTER SEVEN

The return trip to the housing development was much slower than the trip out had been, but Slade didn't mind too much. They'd done good work that day, even if he'd run afoul of a violent vamp who was just too damn fast for him. He'd feel chagrin about that 'til his dying day, but Kate had a few good points. This vamp had to be old if she could transform herself into an innocent-looking bear cub. From all he knew, they usually didn't learn to shift shape until they had a few centuries under their belt.

He'd been prepared to face a demon, not a faster-than-light bloodsucker. Demons, surprisingly, were slower. Even the ones who shapeshifted were confined to near-shifter speeds, regardless of the form they took. Vamps, though, they were in a class by themselves when it came to speed and deadly strength.

Weakened as she was, the bloodletter had still been more than a match for even Slade's skills. He hated admitting there was something out there that was better than him, but he knew it now, for a fact. He'd been given a lesson in humility—in front of witnesses. He'd been able, with Kate's help, to hide the full extent of his embarrassment from the cougars, but he'd had to come clean with the priestess. Much to his everlasting shame.

He had wanted to make a good impression on Kate, not make her feel sympathy for his sorry ass. Way to go to impress the ladies. Smooth, Slade. Real smooth.

When she finally pulled the rented SUV into the housing development, he was relieved. The kitten had woken up but wasn't moving around too much on his lap. It was traumatized from its ordeal, but it seemed comfortable with him. It was purring as he stroked its soft fur with one finger. It was so small. White with little black speckles and so fluffy. He'd never been one for pets, but he'd have to be made of stone not to feel something when faced with a tiny, helpless ball of fluff that purred.

"She likes you," Kate observed, parking the SUV in the driveway of a house he hadn't seen before. It was smaller than some of the others, in a more or less protected position on a cul de sac.

"She's cute," he agreed, scooping the kitten into his palm as he prepared to leave the vehicle. "Is this your place?"

"Yep. Pardon the mess. I'm still not entirely moved in and some of the rooms are a little bare. I have to get more furniture, but I haven't really had time or patience to do it yet."

He didn't comment as he pushed himself out of the vehicle. He didn't want to accept her help to walk the few steps to the front door, but found he had little choice. His ribs were giving him hell and he liked having her close to him even if he didn't like acknowledging his weakness.

He leaned against the side of the vehicle for support while she opened the back door to let the animals out. A few started to wander away under Slade's watchful eye.

"Hey!" he called and the escapees turned to look at him. He was an Alpha and even those stubborn house cats recognized his authority. "Stay with us," he commanded in a quiet, non-threatening tone. He tried to convey the idea that he would protect them and one by one, they came back, sitting attentively at his feet, looking up at him for guidance.

Kate chuckled as she lifted the last of the smaller creatures down from the SUV. "I've never seen a house cat come to heel before. Neat trick."

"To be honest, I wasn't sure it would work. Most felines, even the small ones, have minds of their own, and don't usually follow orders. But there are wolves in this community and these little guys have been traumatized enough. I don't think any of the shifters would hunt house cats with any kind of serious intent, but dogs do like to chase things."

"Good point." She secured the vehicle and came over to put her shoulder under his, supporting him.

She was gentle, but the movement still jarred. He became concerned that maybe he had more than just a couple of broken ribs, but he sucked it up and grit his teeth as they hobbled inside, a parade of little critters following obediently behind.

Her house was welcoming and neat. The living room, which he could see through a large archway as they passed, had a big, comfy-looking couch, but he knew if he got down into those big cushions, he wouldn't be able to get out under his own steam anytime soon. The thing would swallow him whole and he'd need help levering out of the cushy trap.

Kate must have realized it too, because she steered him away from the living room and down the hall.

"I have a guest room down here with its own attached bathroom," she explained as she ushered him toward the back of the house. I think it was originally designed to be used as an office, but I have some elderly friends who I hope will visit. I don't want to make them go up and down those stairs, so I decided to repurpose the place a bit. There's a bed in there already, though not much else, I'm sorry to say."

"I'm sure it's fine," Slade said as they came to the end of the hall and she reached out to open the door. "Anyplace with a flat surface I can stretch out on will be great. Even the floor."

He wasn't kidding. The way his body hurt, he'd settle for the clean hardwood floor if he didn't get to a better spot real soon. There was definitely something more than broken ribs going on inside his torso, judging by the piercing pain flaming through his midsection. Damn.

Kate pushed the door open and Slade saw the room had a little more in it than she'd claimed. There was a nightstand next to the bed with a big-numbered, illuminated alarm clock and a lamp with a flowery shade. An ornate armoire sat along one wall, though it had been only partially built. The frame was up, but the shelving and internal poles and drawers had yet to be put together and inserted. There was also a velvety looking wing chair. It had very feminine lines and looked like an antique reproduction, though Slade didn't know much about furniture.

The bed was queen-sized and had been made with frilly white linens that had little roses and pansies on it that sort of matched the lamp. There were big, fluffy pillows covered with the same fabric and on the walls there were two framed watercolors of pansies and roses. He sensed a theme. A very grandmotherly theme.

"Who exactly where you expecting to stay here?" Slade couldn't keep the amusement from his voice.

Kate looked shy for a moment. Almost embarrassed. She helped him sit on the edge of the bed, then busied herself turning down the comforter and removing some of the mountain of pillows.

"I had a number of teachers along my path. A few of them are older ladies. Priestesses who helped me find my way. They don't travel much, but I wanted to have a comfortable place ready if any of them came to visit."

Slade saw how much it meant to her. "I think any woman would love what you're doing here."

"But not a man?" Kate finally looked up at him as he pet the kitten in his hand who was nuzzling his jacket.

"You have to admit. It is a little... uh... flowery." He looked around and smiled. "But it's pretty. My mom would love this. Pansies are her favorite flower."

They'd lost some of the familiars to other parts of the house, but a few had followed them into the flowery room. One in particular jumped up on the bed and walked right up to Slade, sniffing at him and the kitten in his hand.

"I think we found the kitten's mother," he observed as the female cat began to lick the kitten affectionately. The female cat was black, but the baby was white with little black speckles. Still, they acted like momma and baby to Slade's eyes.

"Looks like that mystery is solved," Kate observed. She stood and got one of the boxes that had held the last few unfinished pieces of the armoire. She then went into the bathroom and came back with a few towels. She spread two out on the bed behind Slade and put one in the box, making a little nest for the cats.

Slade put the kitten into the box when Kate brought it to him. She put the box on the floor and the momma cat hopped down off the bed and joined her baby in the warm nest Kate had created for them.

The doorbell rang and Kate looked toward the hall. "It's Valerie. I recognize her energy." She looked back at Slade and seemed torn about leaving him. That felt both good and bad. Good that she'd want to stay by his side. Bad that she wanted to do it because he was in such bad shape, and she knew it.

Valerie, though, could help with the menagerie that was about to tear up Kate's new house and probably crap all over it too. Slade didn't know much about familiars, but he suspected they'd want food and a place to relieve themselves sooner rather than later.

"Go. I'll be fine. I'm just going to lie down for a few minutes. If you need help, let me know."

He hated admitting his weakness and he really would have preferred playing the protector role and helping with the rescued critters, but she should be safe enough with Valerie. Even though the housing development had been breached to disastrous ends recently, everyone was on high alert now. Slade doubted anyone with malicious intent would be able to sneak up on the shifters now.

Kate still looked worried, biting her lip in a way that made him want to kiss her. Valerie didn't ring the bell again, but they were both well aware that she was waiting.

"Call if you need me," Kate said finally, looking back at him several times as she made her way down the hall.

Slade listened to the door open and relaxed when he heard the women talking. Valerie had brought supplies with her and he could hear them both set to work as soon as the front door closed. All would be well. For now.

Slade made an effort to get out of his clothing, but even the slightest movement hurt like hell. He was winded and in even more pain when he finally decided to just lay down and try not to hurt for a little while. He lowered himself inch by painful inch to the towel-covered bed behind him and left his booted feet hanging off the side. He didn't want to ruin the flowery, feminine sheets Kate and put so much thought into if he could help it.

He'd just rest here for a few minutes first, then he'd figure out what to do next.

Valerie was a godsend. She had litter boxes and the stuff that went inside them, plus a few plush, cushioned beds for the animals that were too traumatized to be moved. To her credit, she did manage to coax the majority of the animals to leave with her, but a few were stubbornly affixed to Kate and would not leave their savior. At least not yet.

Valerie confirmed that all of the animals had been familiars. There was a special quality about such creatures. They were attracted by magic and able to act as companions to mages, grounding them to the earth even as their magic allowed them to touch on realms beyond most human comprehension.

They put those animals that were in the worst shape into small carriers Valerie had brought with her. Her husband, Keith, showed up a few minutes later to help carry them out to his vehicle. For the rest, which were all feline, Valerie helped Kate gather them into one place in the house. They would have freedom to roam around the living room and the long hallway. The rest of the doors were closed and litter boxes were placed in a discrete corner. The cats would have enough places to explore as well as rest while Kate helped Slade.

She knew he had to be in worse shape than he was letting on. His skin was pale and every time he moved, he grimaced involuntarily. He was putting a brave face on it for her benefit, but she knew he was in terrible pain. That vampire had hit him hard. Harder than Kate had ever seen anyone get hit—even in movies. He'd be lucky if ribs were all she had broken.

And his pride was probably even more injured. She got the idea that Slade wasn't the kind of man who liked to show any kind of weakness at all. She would have to examine him for herself to discover the extent of his injuries. He certainly wouldn't be telling her anything he didn't want her to know.

Luckily, Kate had always had a strong affinity for healing. It was one of the things she was particularly good at, and she planned to work her magic on Slade whether he was cooperating or not. She had ways to make him compliant if he dared to argue. He was in her house now. She would treat his wounds and nobody besides the two of them would ever have to know.

When Valerie and Keith left and Kate finally had a chance to check on Slade, she found him asleep on the bed, fully clothed, his legs still hanging over the side. Poor guy.

She approached him cautiously, wary of shifter reflexes. Sure, he didn't look dangerous at the moment, but she'd be smart not to underestimate him.

He didn't even stir as she sat on the bed at his side. He was down for the count.

Kate tried to be gentle as she moved. She'd brought scissors with her to cut off the scraps that remained of his shirt. That would be the easiest way to get him out of it without hurting him more. She set to work, pulling the fabric away from his body and cutting through it, piece by piece.

What was revealed as she worked made her gasp. The vampire's shifted claws had gouged deeply into his skin. In fact, he was still bleeding sluggishly from some of the cuts. Rows of angry red lines covered his torso and she could see where bruises were beginning to form on his side. The same side he'd been clutching as she drove him home.

She didn't bother trying to get his shirt out from under him. She just cut it off around him until his upper body was bare. His pants were bloody, but his legs had fared a lot better. The vampire had been going for his throat and she hadn't damaged him much below the waist.

Still, Kate wanted him as comfortable as possible before she started healing him in earnest, so she paused to take off his boots before going into the bathroom to gather a few things she would need. Her first order of business was to sponge off the blood and clean the cuts as best she could. Magic would go a long way toward fixing him up, but it was always better to start with a clean slate, as it were, before attempting something of this magnitude.

She'd clean him up first, then use more extravagant means to do what she could to make him feel better. That plan in mind, she set to work, using a small basin of warm water and a sponge to get the worst of the blood and even some threads from his clothes, out of his wounds. He shifted a few times, but didn't wake as she worked. She wondered at that. In her limited experience, shifters were very sensitive about people being nearby. They seemed to revel in touch—but usually only from family or friends.

She didn't really fall into the friend category with Slade, did she? They'd only met that day. She would've thought it would take more for him to be so comfortable around her, but then again, maybe not. There certainly had been a strong attraction between them from the moment they'd met. She found herself thinking of him in romantic terms when she knew darn well he was only here to do a job. He wasn't staying. She had to resign herself to that.

Still, as she bathed his muscular torso, she found herself daydreaming just the tiniest bit.

What would it be like to make love with Slade? Would he be rough and masterful? Or would he be gentle and tender? Would he make her scream, and could she make him purr?

She'd never been with a shifter before. In fact, it had been a long time since her last short-lived affair. She had decided to make her life among these big, strong, attractive people, but hadn't been wowed by their physical attributes. They were still people—albeit more spiritual in many cases, than the regular humans she'd been around before. Slade though, he drew her like no other man ever had. She had only known him a few hours and she already wanted to know what he would feel like inside her.

All she had to do was glance in his direction and her thoughts strayed to naughty places. The attraction was instant and intense. She wanted to feel his skin against hers, his body rocking her to completion. And she'd bet her life's savings that the climax Slade could give her would be unlike anything she'd ever experienced. The way their magic met and twined whenever she touched him hinted at it. Theirs would be a joining not soon to be repeated and she wanted it. She wanted *him*. Bad.

So many thoughts raced through her mind as she ran the damp sponge over his muscular chest. She touched him as lightly as she could, not wanting to cause him further pain. The poor man had been through a lot today—both the physical hurt to his body and what had to be hurt to his pride as well.

She moved gently, but soon had him cleaned up enough to begin her real work. Laying aside the basin of bloody water, she rubbed her hands together to focus her energy, then began to work. She held her hands about an inch above his body, moving slowly as she took stock of the places where he was more seriously injured. Diagnosis was a rare skill, but one she had mastered early in her training.

Kate tried to hold back her shock at what she found. Emotion may or may not help her focus her power to best advantage. She had to try for objectivity as she discovered what was truly wrong with him and why he continued to sleep even while she worked on him. She suspected that wasn't normal shifter behavior. From what she'd seen they were always alert, particularly Slade.

She started at the top and worked her way down his torso, pausing when she came to his ribs. She counted four broken ribs—one dangerously close to puncturing his lung. Dear Goddess. She didn't know how he'd been walking around with this kind of damage.

She went deeper and found internal hemorrhaging. Here was the real problem. When the vampire had hit him, she'd dealt him a crushing blow that had bruised his internal organs and caused a great deal of bleeding inside, where he'd been able to hide the extent of his injury through sheer force of will.

The kind of pain he'd hidden was something few people—even shifters—could manage. Most would have passed out long before. Slade had managed not only to stay conscious, but to let her dilly-dally around with the animals before she saw to him.

Guilt ate at her. She should have let the animals wait. Slade was much more badly injured than she would have imagined based on his actions. She couldn't believe he'd waited so long to succumb to the pain, never making a sound about what had to be excruciating.

Her admiration for his control went up another notch, but at the same time, she wished he'd have let on what was really going on. She would have come to him much sooner. As it was, she was going to have a hard time fixing him up. She would. She had to. But these kinds of injuries were tricky.

Focusing, she sent her energy into him in small pulses, aimed at the areas of angry red in her internal vision. Healing required a slightly different use of her magesight. Many could not manage it, but she'd pleased her teachers with her ability. She would need all her skill now to help Slade, but she wouldn't let him suffer any more than he already had. She would heal him if it took everything she had left. He was worth every sacrifice. Such a noble creature—such a pure-hearted man—could not be lost. She prayed the Goddess would not allow such an injustice.

Kate touched him, using her fingers to aim the arrows of healing energy into his body, to the places that needed it most. She stopped the bleeding little by little and used dispersive magic to break up the pooling blood and encourage it to be reabsorbed into his body.

He would probably be weak for a bit while his body made up for the lost blood, but he would be a lot better than he was now. She stopped the last of the bleeding and began to repair the internal injuries as best she could. She could do a lot to speed his recovery, but the fine work would have to be done by his body itself. She could do the heavy lifting—removing the bruising and even giving the bones a head start on fusing—but he would be achy for a while as his internal systems did the rest.

One thing she noticed as she worked was that his magic rose up to meet and help hers. It didn't fight her influence, as had happened sometimes when she tried to work on other shapeshifters. Instead, his inner magic met and augmented hers. That was new. And very useful. She was able to work more quickly and deeper than she had expected with his magic fueling her own. Maybe his healing would be more complete than she'd thought.

It was as if he somehow knew on an unconscious level that she was trying to help him. While it might hurt a bit as she did her work, the ultimate goal was one of healing and his magic seemed to embrace hers and even encourage it.

When she finally sat back and exhaled the breath she'd been holding, she was dizzy. The room spun a little, but it didn't matter when Slade's eyes opened. Slowly, he turned his head and smiled at her, his half-lidded gaze meeting hers with easy intimacy.

Oh, yeah. She had to catch her breath as a startling mix of sexual energy and relief zinged through her.

"How are you feeling?" she asked gently, her throat dry from the exertion of the past half hour.

"Better." His eyes narrowed even as he smiled. "Embarrassed. Thankful."

She smiled at him. "There's nothing to be embarrassed about. You took on an ancient, blood-starved, crazed vampire and lived to tell the tale. From what I hear, that's an uncommon thing." She brushed a strand of his black hair away from his brow. "Slade, you could have died of those injuries. You were bleeding internally and it was..." She had to pause as emotion welled. "It was bad," she finished in a whisper.

Slade made an attempt to get up, but she stilled him, reaching for his hands. He turned the tables on her and pulled her down on top of him until their faces were only inches apart, her fabric-covered breasts flattened against his bare chest.

"Thank you." His simple words whispered against her lips, and she needed to taste him. To know he was alive and with her. Her head lowered a fraction of an inch and then he took control.

His kiss let her know, in no uncertain terms, that he was feeling better. It started out friendly, but soon turned passionate and when he rolled them both to the side, she didn't protest, even though she knew she should caution him to take it easy.

She was too caught up in his kiss, the feel of his arms engulfing her, protecting her, sharing his warmth and the heat of his skin.

She wanted more.

CHAPTER EIGHT

The feel of Kate under him was something Slade had wanted to experience since the first moment he'd seen her. It was even better than anything he'd imagined in the short hours since they'd first met.

Never in his long life had he felt such an instant, compelling attraction to a woman. He'd always been somewhat aloof in affairs of the heart, never spending more than a few weeks with any one woman. Running the other way if they showed signs of becoming too attached to him. Slade had been a loner—a tomcat on the prowl—which wasn't all that uncommon among big cat shifters.

But something about this priestess called to him on a deeper level. He wanted her to become attached to him. Actively wanted that, and so much more, from her.

They hadn't known each other long at all, but he'd heard that sometimes these sorts of things happened. Somehow, their magic recognized each other. Recognized and mingled in the most tantalizing way.

Her magic had reached out and caressed his senses from the moment they started working together, using their power in a harmony he hadn't ever felt with anyone else. She just... fit... somehow. Their power fed off and magnified each other, which was something entirely new to him.

Even his own family—the few who had magic like his—didn't evoke this kind of response. His mother and great-grandmother had taught him how to use his power but theirs had always remained separate and distinct from his own. Their magic competed with his for supremacy—as such things often did in his experience. They had counted him trained when he could copy their example and do whatever task they had set without their magic guiding his.

The few times he had overpowered his mother's attempts to teach him had been uncomfortable tests of will. It was at that point—at a very young age—that his training had been turned over to his great-grandmother. He'd never been able to overcome her magic. At least, not until he was fully adult. They'd never put it to the test, but he believed he was at least his great-grandmother's equal now, if not slightly better. He would never pit his skills directly against hers out of respect, but he'd discovered things about himself and his magic over the years of his adulthood that would probably surprise the old gal.

Kate's magic was different. So beautifully different.

It caressed him on several levels. Spiritually, she was a bright light of the Goddess' favor. She touched Mother Earth and channeled the pure heart of the planet. The music of the spheres sang in her magic and the sheer goodness of the Light shone in her clear eyes.

Her heart was pure. Of that he had no doubt. Whether she had come to her calling already that way, or if she had been purified by the Lady's Light, Slade didn't know. It didn't really matter. She was beautiful inside and out, and to him, she was almost perfect in every way.

She wasn't a shifter, but that didn't really matter in the grand scheme of things. Differences often made partnerships stronger. Slade wasn't a snob. That Kate was a woman of power, a priestess of the Lady, was nice, but he knew he still would have wanted her had she been a powerless mortal with no knowledge of the paranormal world.

One of his relatives had already found a deep and true mating with a human, and Slade didn't turn up his nose at their love. In fact, he admired their relationship, glad of their happiness. It didn't matter to him that the newly adopted member of his Clan would never shift shape. All that mattered was that they loved each other and were happy.

Happiness was rare in this dangerous time. Slade had dedicated his life to ridding the world of those who would cause sorrow. Making the world safer was his mission—in whatever form it took.

This time, his calling had led him here, to this amazing woman and the new feelings she stirred in his soul. He didn't question it too much. He didn't want to jinx whatever it was that had started to grow between them. One should not question a blessing, he had learned.

So rather than question, he merely enjoyed. He'd taken this moment out of time to take Kate in his arms and kiss the living daylights out of her.

She responded so beautifully. She fit so perfectly in his arms. In his bed.

Okay, it wasn't technically his bed, but his aroused body didn't know the difference. It could be the sandy desert floor or the flower covered sheets on the guest room's bed. Wherever he was, as long as Kate was in his arms, he was happy. And seriously turned on.

"Kate," he whispered against her lips, breaking the kiss as the fire building inside him roared higher.

He lowered his mouth to slide over her neck, nipping lightly. He had to hold back his instincts. He wanted to bite. To claim.

But he couldn't. Not yet.

She moaned and any pain he might have still felt from his injuries was wiped away by the sound of her passion. His hands moved over her, looking for fastenings and not really succeeding. The sound of tearing cloth didn't really register over the joy of feeling her bare skin against his hands, against his chest.

He cupped her breasts, ripping the flimsy bra off her shoulders and then pulling until the metal clasps in the back bent or tore off under his power. Even in his rush to get her naked, he was careful not to put any strain against her delicate skin. He'd rather die than hurt her in any way.

The bra came off and then her soft breasts were in his hands, in his mouth, as she writhed against him. Her legs rose and parted, surrounding him with her warmth, encouraging him without words to claim the place he so wanted to go.

He paused, reveling in the feel of her against him. Her breasts were soft, pointed at the tips, ready for him. Excited. Her whole body shivered as he sucked her deep into his mouth, using his tongue to play with her nipple, his other hand mirroring the effect on the other side.

She was so deliciously feminine against his questing fingers and tongue. She tasted divine. Her skin held the flavor of ambrosia to his starved senses. He loved hearing her little sighs and the feel of her trembling beneath him.

But he wanted more. And judging by the way she responded to him, she did too.

Slade's hands moved downward, over her hips. The soft, full skirt she wore was no hindrance to his quest. He blessed her choice in clothing, yanking the soft cotton down over her hips rather than bunching it up around her middle. It would only get in the way later. Coaxing her legs together for a moment, he stretched the elastic waistband of the peasant skirt down and over her long, shapely legs.

She helped, kicking the wad of fabric away from her feet once he pushed it past her knees. Her panties went with it and then she was bare against him. She parted her thighs eagerly as he sought his place between them.

He still wore his pants, but that was easily remedied. What really mattered now was that she wanted the same thing he did. That she was as ready for him as he was for her.

"Kitten, if you want to stop, tell me now." He was a desperate man.

She seemed to be beyond words as her hands sought and found the fastening of his pants. She worked with ferocity, if not a lot of skill, to open his fly and push the offending fabric out of her way. Slade felt a growl rise in his chest—a growl of full-on desire—as he helped her reveal his cock. His undeniable desire for her delectable body.

And then her hand was fisted around him and he had to shut his eyes, the pleasure was so intense. She rubbed and grasped, pulling him toward her. She seemed desperate for what he too wanted above all things in heaven and earth.

He wanted her.

To be inside her. To make love with her. To be the man who brought her pleasure and fulfilled her every desire.

There was no time to lose. No time to wait. Slade moved over her, feeling her wet, eager heat beneath him as her hand withdrew from around his ready cock.

Thank the Goddess. She was ready and oh-so-exquisitely willing.

He slid into her with a sigh of relief and a growl of claim. He was putting his mark upon her—not in obvious ways, but in the ways of his people. His scent would become part of her skin. His magic would touch and blend with her own.

Already he could feel their power combining and twining. Welcoming and intensifying everything between them.

Never had Slade expected to find a woman who could match him on so many levels. And yet... here she was. Beneath him. Around him. Part of him as he was now part of her.

Home.

Slade growled as he realized he had, in all likelihood, found his mate.

"Slade!" Her whispered plea brought him out of the fog of discovery and back to the matter at hand.

Kate wasn't a shifter woman to understand how fast fate could decide the rest of their lives. She would have to be wooed.

And there was no time like the present to begin to impress her with his skill as a lover. The rest would come... in time. He prayed.

Slade moved within her, sparing a moment to tease her clit with one finger while he levered slightly away from her body. He wanted to see these first moments of claiming. To remember them forever. He wanted to bask in the feel, sight and scent of her, of them, together. This moment would change the rest of his life—if he could only convince her of his sincerity.

And his desire. In all likelihood, that would be the easy part. He got hard every time he looked at her. Now that they were together, he wouldn't be shy about letting her know it.

He stroked in and out of her tight sheath, loving the feel of her. His finger played with her clit, and he noted what made her whimper and what made her moan. He loved the little sounds she made as his cock reached the stopping point—inside her as far as he could go. And he soon discovered that little spot inside that made her shiver in ecstasy every time he managed to hit it. He made it his personal goal to hit it as often as possible.

She came around him in a shivering fulfillment as he stroked deeper still, opening to him as her body relaxed into his possession. He lowered his body over her, wanting more. Now that he was certain of her pleasure, he would take a bit for himself.

There would be plenty to go around this night of nights.

"Look at me, Kate," he whispered as he brought his chest over hers, rubbing lightly against her breasts. He felt the renewed excitement in her quivering body, surrounding him, surrendering to him.

She opened her eyes and their gazes met. Held. Merged.

"Slade?" She seemed uncertain, but willing to follow where he led. How did he get so blessed as to have a woman like this? He would thank the Goddess every day for the miracle of Kate.

"Hold on to me, kitten. I'm going to take you again and I don't want you to be afraid. I might bite, but it won't hurt. I promise."

Her smile lit his world as her arms went around his neck, drawing him even closer.

"I know you would never hurt me, Slade. In fact, I really like what you've done so far. Keep going." Her teasing expression challenged him and he liked the fact that she could play with him while he was still hard inside her. Cats liked to play.

Slade lowered his mouth to hers and kissed her while his body began a steady rhythm, picking up speed and power as he went along. His lips strayed down her jaw to her ear, and then to her neck.

As the moment of crisis approached, he knew she was with him once more. Her beautiful body responded so perfectly to his every desire. It was as if she had truly been made just for him.

And perhaps she had been. It was said there was a perfect match for everyone. Slade believed now, beyond the shadow of a doubt, that Kate was it for him.

He nipped the delicate skin of her neck, just at the join where the shoulder began. She seemed to like it, so he bit a little harder. And then... as climax approached, he let loose and truly bit down, drawing a tiny bit of her blood.

The taste of it and the feel of her orgasm brought about his own frenzy. Together, they shouted their pleasure to the heavens as he surged into her one last time. She received all he had to give and gave it back, tenfold.

Pleasure spiraled and peaked like nothing he'd ever felt before. Slade knew, nothing would ever rival this feeling. No woman would ever replace Kate in his heart, his mind, or his bed, forevermore.

Kate napped after the amazing orgasm stole her breath and all her sanity. Slade was like no one and nothing else she'd ever experienced. He was in a class totally by himself. And he'd taken her places she never imagined existed. And wanted to visit again and again.

He had moved them to the center of the big bed, tucking them both under the incongruously frilly blanket and bedspread. His body was hot as a furnace and she knew he probably didn't need the blanket to stay warm, but his actions spoke of his care of her wellbeing. She was only human and he didn't take any chance that she would feel cold.

What a sweetheart of a man. Though if she ever said that to him out loud, he'd probably scoff.

He was a protector. A soldier, yes, but something even deeper inside him made him want to help as well as protect. It seemed to be his very nature. His calling and his birthright.

What a guy. There was nothing she found as attractive as that combination.

Except maybe his haunting blue eyes, spectacular body and handsomely chiseled face.

She ran her hands over his chest, moving slightly so she could see where her fingers were doing the walking. A dark mark low on the skin just under his heart caught her attention. She traced the tattoo with her fingers and wasn't surprised to hear his breathing change from the even, low pace of sleep to the more rapid cadence of wakefulness.

"Why do you have the word *trust* tattooed under your heart?" she asked in a sleepy voice. She was still feeling the slumberous effects of his lovemaking and the whole world had a rosy glow.

"It's a reminder," he answered. His voice was low, intimate, gravely. Sexy.

Rawr.

Her body came alive just thinking about what he'd done to her before. Just like that, she was ready for more.

"A reminder of what?" She had a hard time focusing on the discussion they were having, but she felt it important to understand why he'd mark himself permanently in such a way. It must have great meaning to him, and anything that meant that much to him, she wanted to understand.

"To trust my heart," he said, turning to her and placing soft kisses along her jaw. "It was a lesson I learned young and didn't want to forget."

She wanted to ask what he meant, but his head dipped lower and he took her nipple into his mouth, blotting out all thought of what they'd been talking about. She'd get back to it later... sometime... maybe.

He made a feast of her body, taking time to perform a detailed exploration that made her toes curl and her body yearn for him. He drove her passion higher, laving her skin with that amazingly talented tongue of his. She learned to appreciate his tongue and his hands as he ran them all over her body, arousing, cajoling, enticing.

When he dropped lower, tearing the covers off her as he went, she began to shiver. And when he pushed her legs apart, holding her gaze with those blue, blue eyes, she almost came on the spot. He moved closer, lowering his head but holding her gaze.

And then his tongue delved between her thighs. Slade licked her clit, swirling his tongue around it in heady circles before moving lower, sliding into her passage. He fucked her with his tongue, which penetrated deeper and harder than she had expected.

She'd have to ask him about that. He was a shapeshifter, after all. Maybe he could shift just parts of himself? She wasn't sure. But something extraordinary was definitely going on where his tongue entered and retreated over and over again until she cried out and bucked against him.

Big hands held her thighs, controlling her involuntary movements and keeping the connection between his mouth and her body. Kate had never felt the like.

She gasped for air when he finally released her, stalking up her body to join his mouth to hers. She tasted herself on his lips and felt the rumble of what could only be described as a purr as his chest rubbed against her breasts.

She had just come but already her body was thrumming with renewed arousal. Or maybe it had never left—just been momentarily satisfied but never quenched.

Kate ran her hands over his muscular shoulders and wherever she could reach. His skin was hot against her palms, comforting and somehow protective. She felt like nothing could harm her when she was in his arms. No problem from the outside world could intrude into the space between their straining bodies. There was only room for them. The two of them. Together.

She gasped when he abruptly left her, levering his large body over her for a moment. Then his hands went to her hips and simply lifted, urging her up, positioning her body as if she were a doll. He was so strong. It was a big turn-on for her that he could be so powerful, yet so gentle and careful not to hurt her. He was tempering that great strength for her. Taming the inner beast. Showing her the pussycat inside the wildcat.

He flipped her over and brought her to her knees on the mattress, bent at the waist so that her torso was supported by her arms and her ass was sticking up in the air. He growled low in his throat and the sound turned her on.

"Now that's what I like to see," he rasped behind her. "Warm pussy, ready and waiting for me."

She looked over her shoulder to meet his gaze. Something about him made her feel confident. Daring.

She smiled at him and swayed her hips in invitation.

"So what are you waiting for?" she prompted, wanting to play with fire, to push him just a little bit.

His big hands settled at her hips and he positioned himself behind her.

"If that's the way you feel about it, the wait is over, kitten." He winked at her before sliding home from behind. She cried out at the new sensations. It felt so good this way.

Although, she'd bet every way he chose to take her would feel amazing. He was just that good. She would love testing that theory in every possible position for as long as he was willing to experiment. It could take forever.

And wouldn't that be fun?

He started slow but she couldn't last. Not when he seemed to make certain to rub over her G spot at every stroke. She came twice in small completions, but they weren't enough. He kept going, driving her higher.

His hands came around her body and squeezed her nipples, cupping her breasts. The added pressure and the increase in his pace made her whimper with need on every stroke.

"Slade!" she cried out, wanting him to give her the ecstasy that was just out of her reach. She needed him to take her there, to show her the way to nirvana.

He growled and grunted as he dug into her in short, sharp thrusts that sent her straight over the edge. She screamed this time as she came, nearly blacking out from the exquisite pleasure that went on and on... and on.

She was just barely aware of him holding her throughout the most amazing orgasm of her life and after, tucking her back under the covers, still wrapped tightly in his arms. Sleep claimed her between one sigh of exhausted delight and the next and she knew no more until morning.

CHAPTER NINE

"Much as I'd love to stay here all day and explore this thing between us even more…" Slade stretched like the cat that shared his soul as he yawned. No doubt about it, they were both going to be tired today.

"Yeah, I know. We have a lot of work to do." She sat up and skittered out of the bed before he could grab her.

She was a little self conscious about how she looked—and probably smelled—this morning after the debauchery of the night before. She knew shifter senses were much more acute than human noses, ears and eyes. Cleaning up a bit before facing him seemed the wisest course of action. Kate scooted into the bathroom and shut the door behind her, giggling when she heard him grumble good naturedly on the other side of the door.

Although she didn't normally use the small, downstairs bathroom for her morning wake-up ritual, she had stocked it for guests with all the amenities. She took care of more urgent matters before brushing her teeth and then hopping in the shower for a quick wash.

Well, it was supposed to be a quick wash, but as soon as she pulled the flowery curtain closed, she heard the bathroom door open. A moment later, Slade joined her in the shower, which was in a tub enclosure. There was plenty of room for them both, though the water only sluiced down from the shower head at the faucet end of the tub.

His grin turned her inside out and just like that, she wanted him again. Her thighs felt like rubber after all the unaccustomed exercise of the night before, but nothing mattered when he took her into his arms and kissed her under the warm spray of water.

He turned so that the water fell over his back, only a fine spray of mist getting to her, which made the atmosphere somehow more magical, more intimate. A hint of steam, the touch of mist and the enchanting trickle of water on skin. That was the soundtrack for his renewed seduction this morning.

Personally, she thought she might never be able to hear the sound of a shower the same way again after this experience. At least, she hoped more of that life-altering sex was in store for her this fine, fine morning.

Only a few hours in his bed and she was becoming greedy for more. For all she could get, if truth be told. She would take him any way she could get him. Now, later... forever, if there was any way possible.

But thoughts of the future would come later. For now, she was in his arms and she wanted everything he could give her at this moment. A stolen moment out of time.

Before they had to go back to work. To the very important task ahead of them.

To his credit, Slade took a few moments to soap up her body, sliding repeatedly over her breasts and down between her legs, hitting all the strategic spots in between. He let her rinse before he turned her abruptly in his arms and took her up against the wall.

His hunger was such that it was like they hadn't come together—repeatedly—the night before at all. He was ravenous and she enjoyed being nibbled on and rammed into as if he would never get enough of her.

They came together in shuddering bliss, the warm water cascading around them. Her back was to the wall just to the side of the shower head and the water sluiced down over them like warm raindrops. It was all too much against her sensitive skin and she came again just from the aftermath.

Slade growled low in his throat and grinned at her as his dick hardened once again inside her. Kate had observed all kinds of things about shifter recovery time the night before and was learning even more this morning, much to her continued delight.

Slade didn't even bother shutting off the water before lifting her in his arms and stepping out of the tub. The bathroom was small, but there was a tiny bit of counter space just beside the door. Slade lowered her wet bottom to the countertop, arranging her so that he could continue the onslaught that it seemed had only just begun. Again.

The pace was slower this time. Less urgent. But every bit as arousing. Slade slid into her in long, languid strokes. He kept enough distance between them so he could look down at the spot where he possessed her, encouraging her to watch as well as he took her.

There was no warning before the bathroom door opened with a bang, hitting the wall and causing Kate to jump. Everything happened at once as Slade growled in anger and her bottom slid off the slick, wet countertop. Before she realized what was happening, two strong hands wrapped around her from behind, sparing her a bad fall.

But whose hands were they? Kate looked up over her shoulder and met the startled golden eyes of Steve Redstone.

"Sorry, man. Grif sent me to get you. I didn't realize—"

"Yeah, right. You didn't get the hint from her scent all over my sheets?" Slade was angry but calm, his gaze speculative.

"It's her house. The whole place smells like her. And I didn't really pause to think about it. I was in a hurry." The cougar had the grace to look chagrinned. "Sorry, Kate." He met her gaze as his hands lifted her to get a better grip.

She was suspended, naked and wet, between Slade, who was still balls deep inside her, and Steve, who didn't seem to be in any sort of hurry to leave. Kate felt her fear of falling disappear under first embarrassment, and then... arousal?

Sweet Mother of All. One night with Slade had turned her into a nympho.

Then again, of all the shifters she'd met before encountering Slade—which had changed her for all time—she'd speculated about Steve the most. He was the mysterious brother. The warrior. The Special Operator.

And he was ruggedly handsome in a way that she'd admired. From afar. Never in a million years would she have imagined she'd ever be found naked, in his arms.

"Well, since you're here..." Slade looked speculatively from Kate to Steve and back again, seeming to pick up on her renewed arousal. Her cheeks flamed. How could he miss the way she creamed as she realized Steve's hands were only inches away from her bare breasts.

And Steve seemed to realize it too. He moved closer and she could feel something prodding her lower back through his pants. He was hard and getting harder.

Oh, boy. The question was, how far would Slade let this go? And would she be able to keep up? She honestly had no idea.

"Tell me true, kitten," Slade's voice coaxed as the fingers supporting her bottom began to move as the men readjusted their hold slightly to keep her safely suspended between them. "Are you up for a little play?"

"Play?" Was that her voice? It sounded more like a croak.

"Cats are friskier than most other shifters, doll," Steve's voice sounded from behind her.

Holy shit. He seemed to be not only on board with the deviltry she read in Slade's eyes, but encouraging it. She was in big trouble. Of the most delicious kind. Dare she dip her toes in the forbidden pool?

"Uh, what are you suggesting?" Her mouth was so dry, she had to try a few times to get all the words out.

"Nothing too drastic. We don't have enough time, for one thing. For another, you're mine, kitten," Slade stated with finality. "As long as you remember that, the rest is just fun and games. Are we clear on that point? You're mine." He dipped his head and met her gaze with a steady fire in his mesmerizing blue eyes. "Say it," he ordered in the sexiest whisper she had ever heard.

"I'm yours," she repeated, not daring to argue.

Not *wanting* to argue, for that matter. She liked the hint of something perhaps a little more permanent, if that's what it really was. Her heart hoped against hope that it was, but only time would tell.

"Good girl. For that, how about we let Steve play with your tits? The way his hands are inching closer, I can tell that's what he wants. Is that what you want too, kitten? To let him stroke your breasts and squeeze your nipples while I fuck you?"

She moaned at the scandalous words and the images they formed in her mind. Slade must've taken that as a yes because he gestured with a jerk of his chin and Steve readjusted, leaning back against the small span of wall next to the door he'd opened. He lifted her slightly higher so that she was leaning back against his chest, while Slade stepped closer. She was caught more securely between them now, Slade's hands under her ass as she wrapped her legs around his waist.

Steve moved forward to grasp her breasts, enveloping them with the calloused roughness of his warrior's hands. His arms were under hers and he took a moment to shift first one of her arms up and back, to grasp his shoulders, and then the other. She was able to twist her hands enough to place her hands at the back of his neck and hold on for dear life as Slade began to pound into her, rubbing her back against Steve with every thrust.

He touched her a little rougher than Slade, but he seemed to know just how far to push her. His fingers twisted her nipples lightly, then cupped her full mounds as Slade moved ever faster. She moaned and a moment later, Slade came, spurting hot jets of come inside her, triggering her own orgasm.

She'd already lost count of how many times she'd come for Slade. He seemed to know her body better than she did. And now, he seemed to know her mind as well. He'd somehow realized she'd been attracted to Steve, and when fate had handed the opportunity to tease her with the other man's touch, Slade had been all too ready to go with it.

Fun and games, indeed. Kate had come so hard, it was going to be almost impossible to top anytime soon.

Or so she thought.

"Good girl, kitten, but I think we need to help Steve out a bit," Slade said in a rough voice as he began to recover. He pulled out and lowered her feet gently to the floor. "Don't you want to help poor Steve?"

"What do you have in mind?" She didn't want to sound scared, but she was very afraid that's exactly how she sounded.

Meanwhile, Steve had encircled her torso with his big arms and drawn her back against his chest. His hands still played with her breasts, renewing the fire that had never quite gone out. It seemed her body was capable of more pleasure than she had ever really thought was possible. For Slade, she seemed to become aroused and ready with just a few, well-chosen, intensely hot words.

She wondered idly if he could make her come just from talking to her. It was something to explore later, if they had a later, that is.

"Nothing scary, love, or too drastic," Slade reassured her as he grabbed a few towels from the shelf above the toilet. He threw one on the closed lid and used another to dry off quickly and rub at his cock. To her shock, it was coming alive yet again. "Would you be willing to suck him off?" He let that bald statement hang in the air for just a moment while she tried to overcome first her shock, and then her shocking desire.

Oh, yeah, she wanted to suck Steve off—but only because Slade wanted it. Having him there made all the difference. She wouldn't have even considered it without him.

She was Slade's. That thought kept ringing through her mind for some reason. Even if it was only true for this short period of time, that one thought was uppermost in her mind. She would never seek out another man as long as she was Slade's.

If Slade forsook her at some point...well...she didn't know what she'd do then. She'd have to deal with that heartbreak when it came. For now, she would revel in being his and do whatever he asked of her because she knew he had her pleasure and safety foremost in his mind. She trusted him.

And...maybe...she loved him.

Oh, boy.

Rather than answer in words, Kate nodded, biting her lip. She heard a rumble of a low growl from Steve, who was still behind her. He let her go by slow degrees, allowing some space between them.

"Come here then," Slade ordered and she went to him, stepping into the warm towel he held out for her.

He wrapped her in his arms and in the towel, rubbing lightly to dry her skin, even taking a moment to rub at her wet hair so it wouldn't drip uncomfortably against her skin. When the damp towel—and his hands—reached between her legs, she spread wide for him, allowing him as much access as he wanted.

She almost forgot about Steve being in the small room with them as Slade rubbed first the towel, then his bare finger against her clit, making her gasp.

He turned her in his arms and she saw Steve. He was sitting on the closed lid of the toilet seat, on the folded towel Slade had dropped there. His pants were undone, his fly open and pulled down to mid-thigh, his erection standing tall and proud from a cloud of tawny hair that was sparse enough to be appealing and probably matched the color of his cougar's coat as it matched the clean cut hair on his head.

Steve was... impressive, was the only word she could come up with. He'd raised his T-shirt and she saw a very impressive display of washboard abs. He was every bit as handsome as she'd thought he'd be, but the man behind her, who had dropped the damp towel and now had his hands on her hips, guiding her forward, was the real turn-on in the room.

She'd do anything for Slade. Anything.

That this audacious act would bring her pleasure too was part of why she trusted him. He would never do anything to hurt her or to demean her. She trusted him with her safety, her sexuality and her heart.

Her power flared off his, meshing, joining, teasing and flirting before winding around them both and making each other stronger. They were so compatible on so many levels. Slade would push her to new heights, but they were steps she was willing—very willing—to climb. All she needed was him to show her the way.

Slade pushed downward on her back, indicating how he wanted her to bend over. Was he?

Oh, yes. He was hard and he was going to take her from behind while she went down on Steve's oh-so-impressive cock. She almost came right then and there, just from the thought of it.

But she was made of stronger stuff than that. Right?

Kate bent the way he wanted and set to work. She started out slow, trailing her hands up Steve's lightly haired thighs. The feel of his blond body hair was softer than she'd expected. It was a turn-on. A sensual delight.

She teased his groin with fingers first, then with her breath as she lowered her head to blow a stream of air out of her puckered lips at the very tip of his cock. He squirmed and she felt the power she had over him at that moment. It was a heady feeling.

Almost as heady as the moment Slade slid into her from behind. He timed his gentle thrust to coincide with her opening her mouth over Steve's cock. She took him inside her mouth, as deep as she could take him. She wasn't exactly an expert at giving head, but she'd done it a time or two and picked up a few tricks along the way. Although she couldn't take such a big cock all the way, she did her best to make sure he didn't feel slighted.

She grasped the thick base of his shaft with her hands as her mouth worked over the top half of him, sliding, slipping, licking and sucking as she went. She even nibbled on him gently as one hand dipped to play with his balls.

Slade set up a rhythm, timing his thrusts with her forays to take Steve deeper into her mouth. The double stimulation was amazing and when Steve lowered his hands to pluck at her hanging nipples, she moaned with Steve in her mouth and clenched her pussy around Slade's cock as he thrust deep into her from behind.

Both men groaned and she felt a deep satisfaction rise up from within her deepest feminine heart. This was what it meant to be the Earth Mother. This was the power of the eternal female to bring pleasure and healing to the male.

For this was a healing as well as an extremely naughty fucking. Steve was wounded in his soul by what had been done to his family. He—a warrior—had not been able to safeguard his own mother and Kate knew that had to cut deep.

In a way, this was her way of giving a little comfort, not to mention a lot of pleasure, to him. It wasn't quite the normal way a priestess comforted those who relied on her for guidance, but she'd take it. Steve was a special case. As was Slade.

She felt her healing magic rise up in a form it had never taken before. It went from her, in subtle waves, to Steve's broken heart. It would not heal it completely, but the magic would help him begin the process, if he was receptive.

At the moment, he was very receptive. Kate increased her pace, hollowing her cheeks as she sucked him deep. Slade picked up the pace behind her, sliding in and out in sharp thrusts that made her whimper with need. She was close to coming again and she wanted both of these special men to come with her.

She redoubled her efforts and within moments she felt Steve tense as his seed boiled up. Slade drew her away with a sharp tug as Steve came in long spurts over her breasts. Slade came too, spurting deep inside her yet again as she cried out and came, sobbing as her body quaked in the most exquisite ecstasy.

How long she stood there, supported by Slade's trembling arms, she didn't know. It was Steve who toweled his come off her breasts with gentle motions and a half smile on his handsome face.

He leaned forward and kissed her on the mouth, his tongue tangling with hers for a short moment in what felt like thanks. He kissed her sweetly. It wasn't quite like the way Slade kissed her. Slade was more primal. Steve's kiss was one of tender gratefulness and fledgling happiness. Healing and Light.

What she had tried to give him with her magic. Apparently, on some small level, it had worked. She returned the kiss with a lighter heart.

"I guess we need another shower," Slade observed when Steve let her go. There was no anger or jealousy in his voice. He seemed to understand.

He'd already withdrawn from her body, but he was still supporting her. He had probably noticed the way her knees had turned to rubber, but she was feeling better now. Slade let her go and turned her toward the shower, swatting her playfully on the behind as he pushed her toward the still-running water.

She didn't need further urging. She definitely needed another wash—if she could get her legs to support her.

When she left the shower a few minutes later, Steve was gone and Slade had begun to dress in the other room. She joined him and he pulled her in for a deep, almost drugging kiss before spinning her away to allow her to dress.

"I'm sorry if that took you by surprise," he said in a careful voice. She met his gaze in the mirror and saw the look of concern on his face. "Like Steve said, cats are friskier than other shifters. I hope that's okay with you." He walked over to her and turned her to face him, taking her loosely in his arms. "But I meant what I said, Kate. You're mine. I would never ask anything of you that would hurt you in any way—physically, emotionally or magically."

She smiled up at him and saw the relief enter his expression by slow degrees. She reached up and brushed his dark hair away from his face.

"I know that," she whispered. "I trust you."

That statement hung between them. It was so much more than a simple admission of trust. For trust was something that was sacred to her. To the shifter community as well, from all she'd seen.

For her it meant something deeper as well. Something she couldn't come right out and say—not even to herself—at the moment.

"The same goes for me," Slade replied. His voice was calm, but those magical blue eyes of his flared. She felt the truth of his words. Then his gaze turned devilish. "And you have to admit, that was really hot."

She blushed. She could feel the heat rise in her cheeks. Damn her pale skin.

"It was pretty amazing," she agreed, ducking her head to rest it on his shoulder.

"I don't do stuff like that all the time." He startled her with his words. "Just sometimes. On special occasions, if you will." She looked up at him and found he was laughing.

"That's good to hear because I've never done anything like that before in my entire life. I'm not sure I'd be cut out to do that sort of thing as a steady diet. I'm more a one man woman, I think."

"That's okay by me," he was quick to reassure her. "Consider this morning a one-off. We don't have to invite anyone else to join our fun ever again if that's the way you want it."

"Well..." She was blushing again as she tried to be as honest as possible. "I'm not saying never. I'm just saying, not all the time."

His grin was her reward as he hugged her close. "All right, kitten. Whatever you want. I'll give you all you can handle... When the time is right."

She could live with that.

They hustled through dressing and raided the kitchen for whatever could be eaten quickly, while on the go. They were expected by the Alpha and it wouldn't do to keep him waiting too long. When they were ready to go a few minutes later, Slade remembered the magical chalice from the night before. He asked Kate where it was and what she wanted to do with it.

"I don't want that evil thing in my house," she admitted with a disgusted expression. Slade understood. The feel of the chalice's slimy, blood magic was nauseating. "The Alpha's house is more secure anyway. I'm sure he has a place we can bury this until we figure out how to deal with it once and for all."

She retrieved the bag that held the chalice while Slade found a plastic bag to put it in. He held the crinkly plastic shopping bag open while Kate dumped the bloodstained cloth that held the chalice inside. As camouflage went, the old plastic bag was both cheap and effective. Nobody watching them would know the evil they had trapped inside.

That settled, they set off for the Redstone's home. They were very late, but Steve had gone on ahead to let the Alpha know they were on their way.

CHAPTER TEN

When they finally arrived at the Redstone homestead, Kate felt very conspicuous. Not only were they late, but each of the shapeshifters she passed seemed to sniff her a little longer than usual. The response after that initial sniff varied, but usually involved either a wide-eyed look or a wink, then a quick glance at Slade, who remained at her side throughout. A few nods would pass between the men and then they'd move on.

Something was definitely being communicated, and Kate had a sinking feeling she knew what it was. Somehow, the *were* noses seemed to be able to tell they'd spent most of the night and a good chunk of the morning, fucking like bunnies. She'd taken a shower. *Two* showers. But apparently the soap and water hadn't done much to remove his scent from her skin. She wondered if they could smell Steve on her too and what they must think of *that*.

Blushing, she took a seat next to Slade. He didn't seem in a mood to let her stray too far from his side. While that might annoy her at any other time, she was still feeling rosy and warm from the night — and adventurous morning — they'd spent together. Her affection toward him was growing out of all proportion and her heart wanted to be right where she was. Next to him. Able to reach over and touch him or just lean a little to cause the not-too-innocent rubbing of his leg or arm against hers.

He seemed to feel the same. At least, he seemed to be doing his share of leaning and outright touching. He wasn't grabby or annoying, but his subtle touches made her very aware of him. So much so that she was having a little trouble focusing on what was going on.

Everyone had gathered in the living room, including Steve, who spared her a little wink, but nothing more overt than that, thank goodness. When Grif walked in, she schooled herself to calm down and listen to him. Things in the Clan were too serious right now to screw around, even if she just wanted to bask for a bit longer in the amazing man she'd discovered only yesterday.

Had it really been only yesterday? The thought made her blush as Grif sat down and began speaking. She wouldn't examine how easy she'd been for Slade. Thankfully there were more important matters to devote her energy to at the moment. Still, if this all ended badly, she only had herself and her eagerness to jump into bed with the sexy newcomer to blame.

On that somewhat depressing note, she turned her full attention to the Clan Alpha.

"The prisoner finally woke up around seven this morning," Grif began. "His name is Ethan Abrahamson. He admits he's been running with the *Venifucus* for a while. Before that, he was an *Altor Custodis* watcher."

151

Kate had heard the terms before. Both were ancient societies, but they had very different goals. The *Venifucus* were evil. Hundreds of years ago they had been led by a power hungry sorceress named Elspeth, known as the Destroyer of Worlds. She'd been banished — after a long and hard-fought battle — to the farthest realms. Among priestesses it was believed that Elspeth was of fey origin. That, along with her vast power, made her much more difficult to kill. Which was why she had been banished rather than ended for all time.

That was also why the *Venifucus* who had resurfaced in recent months, were intent on bringing her back to this mortal realm. All those who served the Light were working to keep that from happening. If Elspeth returned to this world, the damage would be incalculable. Death and destruction the likes of which hadn't been seen since ancient times. Frankly, Kate wasn't sure the modern world would survive.

The *Altor Custodis*, by contrast, had been organized to keep tabs on Others of all kinds. They were rumored to keep detailed family trees and histories of shifters of every kind and their agents kept tabs on vampires, noting where they were and what they were doing over the centuries they could exist. The *AC* watched magic users too, Kate had heard, though she wasn't very up to date on the organization. What little she knew about them had been gleaned from conversation with some of her teachers.

Both groups kept exceedingly low profiles and it was hard to know what was truth and what was fiction regarding them. Only in recent months had certain groups of Others had contact with either of the ancient societies. The *Venifucus* had been active in trying to kill Allie, the new mate of the *were* Lords. And it had been discovered that the *Altor Custodis* had been infiltrated by *Venifucus* moles who were using their extensive records to very bad ends. If the former mage who had participated in the murder of the matriarch was part of either organization this whole mess had just gotten even more complicated.

"He claims that his partner talked him into going rogue," Grif went on. "According to Abrahamson, the murder of my mother was an independent action that was neither encouraged nor sanctioned by the *Venifucus*. He claimed the organization didn't even know about it, which I find hard to believe." The cougar Alpha ran one hand through his sandy hair in agitation. "I confess, I find it hard to talk to the man. He seems like an empty shell now, and willing to spill his guts, but I just can't gauge his level of honesty. Plus, I want to rip his throat out every time I realize what he did to my mother."

Grim faces nodded all around. Kate thought she knew how hard this was for Grif, especially. As an unmated male, acting as Alpha to a large group of shifters, he had shared that heavy responsibility with his mother. She had helped him lead their people and had been well loved by all. He'd lost his guiding light. His mother. His helper in the day-to-day running of such a large Clan and construction empire.

She knew he didn't like the word, but Redstone Construction was really becoming an empire of sorts — both business-wise and in the shifter hierarchy. Very few other places in the world had so many shifters of different kinds come together under one man's leadership. Few men were capable of inspiring such a thing. But Grif was that kind of leader. And his mother had helped—in particular, with the females and mates of those who worked for Grif. She would be sorely missed. And if Grif ever found a mate, that woman would have big shoes to fill.

"I can't blame you for that," Slade said in a calm voice, drawing all eyes to him. "With your permission, I'd like to talk to him. And if the priestess would consent..." Slade smiled at her and she felt the warmth of his expression. "There are certain magics that can be applied. We'll know if he's telling the truth."

Slade's gaze went back to Grif, and Kate had to admire the way he handled the situation. It would have been so easy to stir the hornet's nest that was ready to erupt with the slightest miscalculation. Slade seemed to know just what to say and what tone to use. He knew how to handle people.

"I'd be obliged," Grif answered shortly, relief on his features. "We have some regular business to discuss. If you can talk to the man now, perhaps you can report back before we break for lunch. We've put our lives and our business on hold for now but there are certain projects and commitments we need to deal with even during this tragic time."

Taking that as dismissal, Kate stood with Slade. Valerie waited at the archway into the living room and smiled as they approached.

"What's in the bag?" Valerie asked immediately, her eyes glued to the disposable plastic shopping bag Kate held at her side.

"Something I'm not prepared to deal with at the moment. We took an artifact from Abrahamson's home," Kate explained to the witch. "It needs to be kept safe until we can figure out how to neutralize it."

"Yeah," Valerie agreed, gulping as she redirected them to another room upstairs. "Keith will know where to put it. Grif gave him the keys to the kingdom." Valerie's eyes were wide and focused on the bag in a fearful way as they made their way into a side room that was set up as an office.

Keith was at the computer, but stood quickly when they entered. His eyes went to the bag as well. It seemed both mates were very sensitive to dark magic, which was reassuring. None of the other shifters had noticed the energy swirling around the plain plastic bag. At least with Valerie and Keith stationed in the house, someone would be aware if anyone tried to take the chalice.

"Have you got a safe place to put this?" Kate lifted the bag by the handles, noting Keith's wary expression.

"What is it?" Keith seemed duly appalled by the evil power the chalice was putting off.

"A chalice stained with blood. We took it from Abrahamson's house," Slade answered succinctly.

"He was filling it with the vampire's blood when we arrived. I think he was feeding it the blood of the familiars he stole too," Kate added. It was clear from their expressions that the couple shared her abhorrence of such an evil act.

"Gross," Valerie said in a shocked voice.

"I can put it in one of the safes," Keith said in a firm voice. "There's one empty right now that's buried partially in the ground. I think that's probably the best place." He reached for the bag and Kate gave it into his custody.

"Mother Earth will help neutralize its evil," Kate agreed, glad to be rid of it. She knew she would have to come back to it at some point in the future. It had to be dealt with eventually, but they didn't have the time or energy to waste right now.

"And we can put additional protective and camouflaging spells on it so nobody of bad intent can find it," Valerie added helpfully.

"That's good enough for me," Kate said, her spirits brightening the tiniest bit to have that burden off her shoulders for the moment. "Thanks."

They left Keith holding the bag—Kate snickered inwardly at that thought—and Valerie took them down to the basement. For the time being, they were keeping Ethan Abrahamson in the underground complex of rooms the Redstones had hidden beneath their home.

Valerie introduced them to a shifter named Max who was stationed in the hallway outside a very plain looking door. Kate knew Max was one of the Alpha's most trusted lieutenants. No doubt he was on guard duty. He opened the locked door for them, using a key he kept on a long chain around his neck. The chain, Kate observed, would probably stay around his neck regardless of what form he took.

When the door opened, they saw Abrahamson lying fully-clothed, in bed, in what looked like a guest room. The room itself was a rather Spartan affair. Bed, table, chair, lamp, desk. That's about all, though it had an attached bath and most notably—a door that locked from the outside. Interesting.

If this was shifter jail, it wasn't too bad by Geneva Convention standards. She might've expected a barred cage considering these people could turn into wild animals, but judging by this small, windowless suite, the Redstones didn't go in for such extremes.

When the door opened, Abrahamson sat up and swung his legs down over the side of the narrow bed. His expression was blank. His face pale in the extreme. He seemed dazed from what had happened the night before and a little...blank, was the best word she could come up with.

Kate extended her magic and found not the faintest spark of magical energy left in Abrahamson. He'd been wiped clean by the Lady's power. Kate had known it intellectually, but faced with the result of her actions last night in the cold light of day, she felt both justified and appalled.

She knew she'd done the right thing. The man had been a monster. But he seemed so pathetic now.

Perhaps that was his true punishment. To exist with the knowledge of Others. It had to hurt to realize that he had once had a large amount of personal magic, and to know it was all gone. Forever denied him because of his evil actions. A lifetime worth of regret and self-disgust. Would it make up for the horrors he had committed? Probably not, but it was a start.

Kate sensed the shifters would have rather had a more permanent and bloody retribution on the man, but they needed to know what he could tell them. There was someone still out there who was potentially even worse than Ethan Abrahamson. And the sorceress who had been his partner in crime still had a piece of the matriarch's pelt. She could not be allowed to keep it under any circumstances. Using it in some evil ceremony was out of the question. So much harm could be done to the Redstones and all who had come into contact with the matriarch over her many years... It was unthinkable.

"I thought I imagined you." The prisoner spoke out of the blue, startling Kate. He was looking right at her, no discernible expression on his pale face.

"Nope. I'm real," she answered, not knowing what else to say.

"You sent the Light. It worked through you." His eyes took on an eerie cast. Like someone who had gazed too long at the sun and seen the wisdom in its burning heart.

"I did as I am called to do. I serve the Light," she affirmed.

"I didn't." His gaze dropped to his hands.

"No, Ethan, you didn't." Slade entered the conversation, moving to stand at Kate's side. "You killed a very important woman. She had many children and people who loved her. They want you dead."

Slade's bald statement lay between them for a moment before Abrahamson looked up, meeting Slade's eyes.

"I don't blame them. It was wrong. But I didn't kill her. I helped, but I didn't do the actual deed. That should count for something."

"That's probably the only reason you're still breathing," Slade said in a calm tone. "Her sons want to rip you apart."

"I know." No inflection. No emotion. Just the flat statement of knowledge.

Kate was learning something important here. The result of what she had done to this guy was downright creepy.

"You have no magic," she stated, needing to be sure he understood simple concepts. "It will not ever come back. Not if you don't embrace the Light. And even then, the Lady will judge you. She may or may not allow you to ever feel the tingle of magic again."

"I know that too," Abrahamson answered quickly, shooting her a glance. "Probably a lot better than you."

Ah. There it was. Finally, a show of emotion.

"We have some questions for you," Slade put in, changing the topic and drawing Abrahamson's gaze.

"Ask away. I have nothing left to lose. I'll answer what I can."

Slade glanced at her and nodded slightly. Kate drew on her magic and set up the protections that would tell her if Abrahamson was lying or evading.

Kate's magic lit the room with a golden glow to Slade's sight. The feel of her power was something he'd always enjoy. It tingled along his senses like a caress. He took a moment to appreciate it before he set to work. With her help it would be comparatively easy to discover what the man knew, if anything, that could be of use to them.

"Who killed the Redstone Clan matriarch?" Slade didn't waste time. He got right to the heart of the matter.

"Not me. I told you. I helped her get here and lure the old woman outside, but I didn't do the actual deed." Abrahamson's tone was flat as he stared into the distance, but Kate's magic revealed the truth in his words. So far, so good.

"You participated in murder. That makes you as guilty as the one who did the actual killing," Slade argued. "Now, tell me her name."

"Sh—" the man began, but something seemed to stop him. Dark magic reared up but Kate's Light blocked it.

"She put a geas on him," Kate muttered. "Looks like it included a prohibition against speaking her name."

"It survived your purge?" Slade was surprised anything could withstand the strength of the Lady's Light.

"Apparently. I don't think it was part of him, but instead, something put on him. It was probably passive until you asked him to speak the sorceress's name. It's her magic. Not his. Dormant until this moment."

"Can you break it?" Slade asked quickly, noting the changing, challenging magics flying all around.

"I think I can keep it from killing him. More than that, I can't promise," she said, strain in her voice as she concentrated on her power.

"Hold it, then," Slade instructed, already looking for a way to break the hold of the sorceress's spell on Abrahamson.

He studied the wavering magical threads and realized they were just that—threads of power—leading back to Abrahamson's heart. A hard enough tug, triggered by his attempts to speak the woman's name, would probably kill him.

But Slade was well equipped to cut such magical bindings.

"Hold steady," he advised Kate, never taking his eyes off the prisoner and the dark magical threads. "I'm going to try something."

He called on his own power and partially shifted one hand to its alternate form. Speckled fur covered his hand and long claws reached out from a large paw.

Kate didn't seem to notice at first, so caught up in her own battle to hold the evil power at bay. When Slade reached out to claw through the ties of dark magic, she jumped a little, catching sight of his clawed hand. To her credit, her magic didn't waver though he knew he'd surprised her.

He cut through the magical ties quickly and Kate did her thing, redirecting the dark power into the cleansing earth beneath the basement. Transmuting it into simple energy and dispersing it. The sorceress's spell was broken.

Slade retracted his arm and shifted it back to a human hand. Kate watched with questions clear in her eyes, but this wasn't the time or place. He'd revealed something just now that few people knew and even fewer understood. Kate had just witnessed one of his secrets and he was sure she had questions, which they'd get to in time. For now, they had a prisoner to finish interrogating.

Personal discussion about the glowing white fur he'd revealed to her would come later. For the paw he'd used wasn't from the black panther he usually showed the world when he shifted, but something much rarer. Something that was his alone. A birthright he didn't dare claim very often.

For alone among all these shifters, only Slade could take more than one alternate form. He showed the shifter world the black panther he claimed from his father's line, but only very rarely did he let the supremely magical snowcat he had inherited from his great-grandmother come out to play.

"The geas is gone. Broken and dispersed," Kate reported with satisfaction in her voice after she'd had a moment to deal with the excess magic.

Slade nodded at her and saw the questions she was repressing in her expression. They would talk. Later. For now, he had to get whatever information he could out of the prisoner.

"We have the chalice," Slade said conversationally, gauging the man's responses both magically and mundanely. He had yet to establish a baseline from which to judge Abrahamson's answers.

"What about the vampire? Is she dead?" Abrahamson answered Slade's question with one of his own. Cagey, Slade thought.

"Is that why you sent us after the chalice?" Kate asked quietly. "Because you wanted her to attack us?"

Abrahamson's eyes narrowed as he looked over at Kate. "I just didn't want her to have it."

"The bloodletter?" Slade asked, surprised. From what he'd seen, the vampire had wanted nothing to do with the evil cup that had held her own blood.

"Her?" Abrahamson looked confused for a moment. "No. She couldn't do anything with it. I meant Sheila. I don't want her to have it."

"Is Sheila the sorceress who killed the cougar matriarch with you?" Slade asked smoothly.

"I didn't kill the cougar. I told you. Sheila did. She did the blade work. She took the fur. I was just along for the ride. Like I always am with her. She's a bitch."

Abrahamson's expression was disgusted. "A bitch with too much power for her own good."

"And that's why you didn't want her to have the chalice," Kate concluded. "You didn't want her to have all that power."

"You should be thanking me," Abrahamson declared. "You have no idea what that bitch is capable of. Or what she's planning."

"Why don't you tell us?" Slade put in, leaning back against the wall as if making himself comfortable.

In reality, he was anything but relaxed. This was information they needed to know. With Kate's influence, he knew they were hearing the truth, and it wasn't good. Even so, they needed to hear it.

Kate might not be aware of it, but there were recording devices cleverly hidden in this room. Slade could hear the slight mechanical hum of them behind the walls. No doubt the cougars upstairs were watching and listening to this interrogation, live, as it happened.

"Sheila wants to expose shifters. She wants humans to know about you animals and join in the hunt. She wants to make your lives hell." The venom in Abrahamson's voice was hard to endure, but Slade made himself listen and not react.

"Is this something the *Venifucus,* as a group, is plotting?" Kate asked, her tone sounding worried to Slade's ears.

"Nah," Abrahamson laughed. "She went rogue. She's not listening to them anymore. She doesn't want to wait for the second coming of Elspeth. She wants the power now. For herself. Sheila is planning a ritual of her own making, and has been gathering the things she needs for weeks now. The pelt was the second-to-last item. There's just one more thing she needs, and then she'll be able to do the ritual—or she would have been able to, if she still had access to my chalice and the blood I was feeding it." Abrahamson cackled then, his laugh sounding eerily through the small room.

"What are the other items she's gathered?" Kate asked, bringing Abrahamson back to the point.

"She wanted something from each of the shifter races living here. We got the blood of a werewolf by paying a biker to pick a bar fight with one, then we scraped some of the shifter's blood off the guy's knuckles while he was out cold. That was the easiest," Abrahamson said with a hint of pride in his actions. "She settled on gathering the scat of a bear shifter since they're too hard to face straight on. We had to hunt in the woods for a long time before we found the right kind of feces. The magical kind." Abrahamson chuckled. "That was a shitty job."

"I bet," Slade agreed, to keep the man talking.

"Actually, that was the part I liked best. I liked seeing Sheila poking around in shit and imagining pushing her face into a big, steaming pile—"

"What else did she need for her plan?" Slade interrupted, not wanting to hear about his sadistic fantasies.

"Well, she tracked the old lady cougar for a week or two and finally arrived at the idea of subduing her in the back garden while her guard was down. It was risky, but between the two of us, we had the magic to pull it off. I didn't know Sheila meant to kill the old gal. Honestly. Until we were there, doing it, I don't think Sheila even realized how easily she could kill her. And once the lady went furry on us, Sheila wanted the pelt. There was no stopping her."

"Not that you even tried," Slade put in, disgusted by what he was hearing, but needing to hear it all.

"No," Abrahamson looked up, meeting Slade's eyes. "Not that I even tried."

"Is that it?" Kate said after a long moment of silence had passed. "Those three items, plus the blood of the magical familiars and the vampire you were collecting in your chalice?"

"The magical blood—and especially the vampire's—was used to make that chalice into something Sheila could use to focus all the items she'd gathered. It's a vessel for the ritual. The only vessel of power available to her in this area. Without it, she won't have nearly as much chance of accomplishing her goal, but she doesn't know you have it yet," Abrahamson said with a crafty smile that sickened Slade. "She'll still be looking for the last item to complete her set."

"And that is?" Slade asked quickly, wanting to be done with this. The guy made his skin crawl.

"She needs something from a raptor. A feather, if possible," Abrahamson said slowly. "And she knows where the raptors who work for Redstone hang out. She knows they walk the iron at night. She intends to knock one down, forcing him to shift, and then capture him in bird form."

"Capture… or kill?" Kate insisted.

Abrahamson shrugged. "Either will work. As long as she gets the feather. But I wouldn't put it past her to want blood too. She liked killing the old lady. I could tell, Sheila really got off on it."

None of this was good news to Slade. Not that he'd expected to hear anything positive from the prisoner. Still, he knew it was time to make a few calls. He just might need some of that backup the Lords had promised was available.

CHAPTER ELEVEN

Slade made his calls quickly and set about pre-positioning some of the guys from the Wyoming Spec Ops group. He knew their leader, a former Army Special Operator named Jesse Moore. Jesse's little brother, Jason, was the Pack Alpha for one of the more influential wolf Packs in the country, thanks in part to the elite group of men who congregated around Jesse.

When shifter warriors retired from the service, quite a few of them found their way to Jesse's mountain in Wyoming. From that home base, Jesse Moore ran an outfit that could be hired by the right people or used to help shifters anywhere in the world, at the Lords' command.

Slade had been told that Jesse was away on a mission of his own at the moment, but one of the more senior guys was authorized to send anyone and everyone they needed to Nevada. Slade spent a very lucrative twenty minutes on the phone, going through the lists of who was available and deciding just who he might need.

Moore's group wasn't solely made up of wolves. There were cats of all kinds, raptors, and even a few bears — black, brown, and even a grizzly with more kills to his credit than all the other bears combined. Slade picked men he knew from prior experience or by reputation. He could rely on Moore's people to get themselves to Nevada as quickly as possible.

It didn't take much to figure out the sorceress's target location. Grif told Slade there was only one site Redstone Construction was involved in at the moment that involved iron work. In fact, according to the Clan Alpha, all the raptors who worked for Redstone were on that project, and had been for the past few weeks.

"Any of your guys have military experience?" Slade asked as they were planning their next moves.

Once again, the group had gathered in the Redstone living room to discuss what they had learned from questioning Abrahamson. As Slade had guessed, the Redstone brothers had been watching and listening via hidden cameras while the interrogation had been taking place.

What they didn't know, and couldn't find out from simply watching or listening, was Slade and Kate's impressions of the truthfulness of Abrahamson's statements.

"A few," Grif answered. "Some of the hawks were in the service but didn't want to continue that life when they got out. Same goes for a few of the wolves. And the Esteban brothers were a sniper-spotter team. They're coyote."

"Bill the tiger was in Viet Nam," Steve added. "And the new bear, Vinnie Maldonado, served in the Gulf."

"Are they on the night shift?" Slade asked pointedly.

"If they aren't, they are now," Grif answered with grim determination, directing his brother Robert to make note of all the names.

"Good." Slade looked around, wondering how his next revelation would be taken. "I've called in the cavalry. They'll be here in a couple of hours and will pre-position themselves out of sight for the most part. I would like to bring a few of them inside the perimeter, disguised as workers. I'd rather have trained soldiers in place on the ground than some of the younger and more inexperienced members of your crew."

Everyone looked at Grif to see what his reaction would be.

"Who did you call?" Grif seemed to be withholding judgment.

"The Ghost Squad." Slade used one of the more popular nicknames Jesse's group had earned with their covert activities.

"Moore's guys?" Grif's eyebrows rose as he considered. Then he nodded. "Good. I served with some of them. So did Steve." Grif looked over at his brother and they both seemed pleased in a determined sort of way.

"That'll work," Steve agreed. "And it'll get some of our people who don't know how to handle themselves in a firefight, out of the way. Not that I'm expecting a conventional firefight, but we really don't know what kind of attack this woman will mount. For all we know, she could have hired a team of mercs."

"Or she could lob a couple of magical fireballs," Kate put in. "She probably has that kind of power, judging by what she's done so far. At least trained soldiers will know how to duck at appropriate times, right?"

Her observation brought a small moment of humor to the otherwise very serious meeting of minds. Slade was intrigued to see the way she handled herself around Steve after their encounter this morning. Outwardly, she was calm and professional. Her magic had spiked a little when she'd first seen Steve, but other than that, both her magic and her casual touches were Slade's alone.

Every time their hands touched, her magic reached out toward him in the most delicious way. He didn't see a single tendril of her power reaching toward Steve, much to his satisfaction. She was attracted to Steve, but not half as much as she wanted to be with Slade. That made him want to pound his chest and howl in pleasure.

Steve was more talkative than he had been before around Kate. He seemed more at ease with her, but still very respectful—just friendlier—which Slade figured was a good thing. It was clear Steve knew the score. He was a cat after all. He was just as frisky as Slade— maybe more so. He wouldn't trespass on Slade's budding relationship with Kate, but he might make a good third from time to time. Slade tucked that thought away and turned his attention back to the problem at hand.

They spent the rest of the morning and part of the afternoon working on their defense plan. Lunch was spent eating and making calls.

Everyone seemed to agree that the sorceress would attack at night, when her power was strongest. Women ruled the night and dark magic enjoyed the darkest hours of the night. Kate had agreed. The woman would make her move in the dark, but exactly what night she would choose, nobody knew.

Slade chose to act as if tonight was the night. If nothing happened, so much the better. They'd be doubly prepared for tomorrow night. But if, by chance, she showed up this evening, they'd be ready.

The building site was down near the famous Las Vegas strip. It was a new mega hotel complex. The tallest of the planned buildings was going up first, and was already well over two dozen stories, with more being added each day. Work on the remaining buildings in the complex was slated to begin in the coming months, according to a schedule that would bring them all into working order around the same time, for a grand opening.

For right now, though, there was only the giant iron skeleton of the tall building at the heart of the construction site.

And lots of space around it where the sorceress could hide.

"I called the site manager," Grif reported as he met them at the construction site. They'd taken separate vehicles, Slade following the Alpha and two of his brothers.

Slade had wanted everyone to stay back at the Redstone home and let him handle the situation, but Grif—predictably—had insisted on coming along. So had Kate, and Slade agreed reluctantly, knowing her magic could be of great help. The sorceress they were going up against had already proven herself to be both powerful and cunning.

"Our man hasn't seen anything yet," Grif reported. "He's already sent home anyone who didn't get the message earlier and arranged for one of the critical pieces of equipment to break down so he could reasonably cancel some of the higher risk work tonight. The largest and most skilled of the raptors are up on the beams and some of Moore's guys have started arriving. They're setting themselves up around the site."

"Sounds good. Did anyone get hold of the raptor Alpha?" Slade asked.

While the Redstones had been interfacing with their Clan, Slade had been delivering a status update to the Lords via his cell phone during the drive here. That, and getting input from Allie and Betina. He'd used the speaker in his rented SUV so Kate could be part of the strategy session for how to deal with the magical side of things.

Slade had also gotten a status update from the Ghost Squad. They had arrived in Nevada and were already on the move. Grif's site manager only confirmed what Slade had known. The Spec Ops guys were good to go and already taking up their positions.

Normally, Slade would have preferred to take care of everything himself, but Kate was a very necessary part of this mission. He hated putting her in danger, but in this case, he knew it was necessary—even vital. She could be of great help, as she had been with Abrahamson. She too, had an important role to play, he suspected.

There was far more on the line here than just the few shifters involved, or even just those many shifters who worked for Redstone Construction. The fate of all shifters, everywhere, could be in question here tonight. If the sorceress succeeded in revealing the existence of the *were*, the fallout could be astronomical. And very, very deadly.

Slade thought it oddly poetic that he'd been sent here to prevent the Redstones from unintentionally revealing themselves out of grief. In reality, the task was much more complicated. The sorceress not only wanted shifters to be outed, but was doing all in her vast power to make it happen.

Grif cleared his throat and recaptured Slade's attention. "Rick Blackwing is the highest ranking raptor here tonight. His father is still the official Alpha, but Pablo retired from the work crews and is away, visiting his new granddaughter in Phoenix right now. So Rick is handling things here," Grif said as he stowed his denim jacket in the back of his truck. His brothers, Steve and Robert, were doing the same, eliminating as much fabric as possible in case they wanted to shift form. "When on the ground, they're going to gather in one trailer and keep track of everyone. I don't want too many raptors running around where the sorceress might be able to corner someone."

Grif had led their little convoy past the gates and into a large temporary building that was used as a private garage of sorts on the vast property. Slade understood the need for a windowless space that backed up to a spot of dense vegetation. *Were* could shift in here and go out the back in their animal forms.

"How about the perimeter?" Slade asked.

He was talking across the hoods of the two vehicles as Kate moved slightly away, trying to concentrate on the magic they both felt at the site. It would take a few minutes to separate out the different strands of shifter magic to be able to see if there was some kind of infiltration. Maybe. There was no guarantee that tactic would work, which was why Slade wanted to do a visual inspection. And his leopard form was best for that.

"We'll check it now," Steve volunteered, already shucking his shirt.

"I noticed several dark areas as we came in, where you guys will stand out. How about you take the dim areas where the brown of your fur will blend, and leave the dark spots to me?" Slade suggested.

"Sounds like a plan. Meet back here in ten?" Steve asked, including his brother Robert in the query. Nods all around firmed the decision.

A moment later, two sand-colored cougars prowled out the back of the big, steel garage.

Kate came to Slade, delaying his shift. There were still a few magical things to settle before he changed.

"Anything yet?" he asked, taking her shoulders in his hands because he just couldn't resist touching her.

"No." She scowled, clearly still concentrating and annoyed she hadn't been able to find the sorceress's trail yet.

"Keep trying, but don't strain too much. I'll help you when I get back. Stay with Grif and help him coordinate things. I'll be back in ten minutes."

He leaned in and kissed her briefly before placing her away from him.

"Be careful, Slade," she whispered.

He looked at her as the change took him and spared a moment to rub his black fur up against her legs and hip before bounding off after the two cougars, out the hidden back door of the garage.

Seeing Slade's panther form was impressive to say the least. He was so casual about his ability to shapeshift, but it was still a miracle to her. Even living among the Redstones and the large collection of shifters they'd gathered around them, she still found it amazing, what these people could do.

Unlike the others, Slade hadn't needed to undress before shifting. Whatever he was allowed his clothing to go into shift with him. They simply disappeared when he took his animal form. That wasn't like any shifter she'd ever heard of or seen. She'd been told — and had witnessed since joining the Redstone's group — that they had to undress first or risk destroying all their clothing. It simply didn't shift with them. Not the way Slade's seemed to.

She hadn't known what to expect from Slade's beast form. The speckled white paw she'd seen before, when they were dealing with Abrahamson, had been quite different from the black on black pattern of his leopard coat. He was dark as midnight, with those fascinating, glowing blue eyes. The same blue, blue eyes that looked back at her from his handsome, human face. The eyes she'd fallen in love with.

Oh, boy. Was she really in love with him? Sadly, for her heart's sake, the answer was a resounding yes.

And his eyes were only the beginning of what she loved about him. He was smart and intellectually sharp in a way that challenged her. He had secrets — of that she had no doubt — but she thought she knew the goodness of his heart, the purity of his soul. His magic had shown that to her. His magic and his actions since his arrival.

Those beautiful, magnetic blue eyes, and the ruggedly handsome package they came with were only the tip of the iceberg. Inside, where it really counted, he was just as beautiful. Even more so.

But the eyes were definitely mesmerizing, regardless of his form. The past minutes—seeing the blue against his black fur—had only driven that point home beyond the shadow of a doubt.

One thing she'd come to learn about shifters—no matter what shape they took, for the most part, their eyes remained the same. Although…now that she thought about it, she'd never really gotten very good look at a hawk or eagle shifter in their bird forms. She wondered idly if their avian eyes would retain the same characteristics of their human forms. It was something to ponder. When she had time.

Right now, there was no time to waste.

Grif was on the phone again, coordinating his employees through the site manager, in order to keep them as safe as possible. He snapped the small cell phone shut and faced her.

"What have you got? Anything?"

She shook her head. "Not a lot. There's a great deal of magic here, but most of it is from your own people. Shifters have a magical signature that leaves traces wherever they go, if you know what to look for. Since I need to open my senses completely, all the traces from your workers are creating quite a muddle of magical threads for me to poke through. So far, I haven't been able to find the one thread that might be the sorceress, but I'm still working on it."

"Can the leopard help?" Grif asked, narrowing his eyes.

"Slade? Oh, yeah, he can definitely help. He has a way of untangling things. When he comes back, we can join forces. Until then, I can lay the groundwork, eliminating anything I can identify as safe, and narrow down the possibilities. I will say this—" She rubbed at her temples. "I don't see anything overtly evil. If she's here, she's hiding her presence really well."

"It's still early," Grif said, tilting his head as he considered. "Dusk is a good time to get into position and wait until the wee, small hours to do the real dirty work."

"Sounds like you have some experience with that sort of thing," she ventured. For all that she'd been living among Grif's people for a while, the cougar Alpha was still very much a mystery to her.

"Both Steve and I served in Special Forces," Grif admitted quietly. "We've done our fair share of covert ops, but something tells me the leopard has us all beat."

"Slade?" Kate looked toward the hidden door where he'd disappeared after turning into the most beautiful big cat she'd ever seen.

"There's no prohibition against it if you want to get involved with him." Grif's words shocked her gaze back to his.

Kate had to smile ruefully. She'd never been very good at hiding her emotions.

"That obvious, huh?"

"Only to a shifter, probably," Grif admitted, leaning against the hood of his truck. "We can smell him on you and vice versa. He knew we would, and he's made no effort to hide your involvement, which means he's serious."

"You can infer all of that just from the way we smell and act around each other?"

Grif actually cracked a small grin. "That, and a lot more. I'm holding back in deference to your human sensibilities."

She had to laugh. "Well, thanks for that." She was distinctly uncomfortable with the idea. She valued her privacy and hadn't quite realized how much of that she would be giving up by moving to live among shifters.

A slight brushing sound made Kate look toward the hidden door and sure enough, the three big cats were returning. The Redstone brothers remained in their animal form while Slade stalked forward, shifting as he moved until he was once again human, clad in his black clothing.

Grif whistled through his teeth. "That's a neat trick. I'd give my left nut to be able to take my clothes with me into the shift. How the hell do you do that?"

"Sorry, Alpha. It's not something that can be learned. It's both magic and heredity. Most of my family can do it, but not a lot of other shifters I've known." Slade stopped at Kate's side, standing in front of the vehicles facing Grif and his brothers. "The perimeter hasn't been breached anyplace we can see," Slade reported. "I'd say there's a ninety percent chance that we beat her to it. She's not here yet—or at least not in position inside the site yet. I also scented a few of Moore's guys outside the fence. They're well hidden. I'd estimate that, given the size of this place, she'd have to be inside the perimeter to be effective. Magic has distance limitations. Even the most powerful of mages usually need to be pretty close to their targets in order to cast their spells."

A subtle knock sounded near the large garage door. A moment later, a man in dark, dusty clothing entered through the man-door at the side of the building.

"Alpha Redstone?" The newcomer greeted Grif first, walking right up to him. "I'm Johan Hager."

Griffon extended his hand to the other man, cocking his head in question.

"I came with the group from Wyoming," he explained in vague terms, probably unsure of how much he could say in front of everyone, and in this location.

"The building is secure," Grif told him. "You can speak freely in front of my brothers," he gestured to the two cats prowling behind him. "This is Kate, our priestess, and Slade, who was sent here by the Lords."

Johan nodded at each in turn. "It is good to meet you, though of course, not under present circumstances. I am a healer and am sometimes called upon to travel with the team in special circumstances." He reached into his pocket and produced three small earpieces, handing them to Grif. "These are for you. I assume you know what to do with them."

Grif took the small devices and passed one to Slade and put one on top of Steve's jacket, hanging over the side of his truck.

"We do," Grif agreed, already placing the small earpiece into his ear. Slade did the same.

Johan's icy gray eyes were almost as intense as Slade's but his blond hair and pale skin made him look completely different. He was also considerably older.

Both Slade and Grif started talking on the small radios they'd been given and Kate found herself under the older man's scrutiny. He smiled at her and she felt pinned by the pale blueness of his gaze. It wasn't entirely comfortable and she started to fidget.

"Fear not, young priestess, all will be well." His comforting words and fatherly tones made her narrow her eyes.

"How can you be so sure?"

"Trust in the leopard." With that inscrutable answer, the man left the way he had come.

He was decked out like a construction worker, so Kate assumed he was returning to his fake duties outside on the site. Something about the man's clear, gray-blue eyes continued to haunt her even after he was gone from sight.

Kate turned back to Slade and Grif. They were both speaking, in turns, with whoever was on the other end of those little radios, finalizing plans and getting updates. After they had everything settled, Slade turned off his mic and came to her side.

"We're going to walk the site and look for any telltale dark magic. Everybody else will be looking for physical signs of the sorceress's presence while we search for the arcane ones." Slade turned back to Grif. "Alpha, your talents are best used in coordination and camouflage for now. Once we locate the sorceress, Kate and I will close in on her. I need you to keep everyone else back, far away from us, while we deal with her. Set up a perimeter in case we fail. Only the raptor she's targeting should be in danger if we do this right and if we can coax her into trying for the Alpha bird, his strength of will and flying ability should help protect him even if we screw up."

"But the right of the kill is mine." Grif was adamant about that one, bloodthirsty fact.

"I do not dispute it," Slade answered firmly. "But if we can capture her — if Kate can defang her the way she did Abrahamson — she could be a valuable prisoner."

Grif seemed to struggle with that idea. He growled deep in his throat and turned away, pacing. The two cougars behind him weren't any happier.

"I allowed that bastard Abrahamson to live, though it went against the grain. I want them both dead for what they did to our mother."

"Could you kill Abrahamson now, in cold blood, the way he is?" Slade asked in a quiet voice. Kate found she was holding her breath, waiting for Grif's answer.

"You bastard. You know I can't. If I could, he'd already be dead. You left him an empty shell, Kate, and totally fucked up my revenge."

Kate was relieved to see the barest hint of humor in Grif's gaze as he looked at her. She didn't mind the profanity, though it was a mark of how upset he was that he'd slipped and used such language in front of her. In her experience, though the shifters were rough and tumble, they were also gentlemen when it came to her. They treated her with respect, from the youngest cub to the roughest warrior. None of them used bad language if they thought she was within earshot.

"Sorry, Alpha," she answered with a shrug of her shoulders. "It was the only way in that particular case. It was what the Lady led me to do."

"I'm not chastising you, priestess," Grif said finally, some of the tension leaving his shoulders. "And it will probably be helpful to have Abrahamson around for a while so we can pick his brain and learn everything he knows about our enemy. But the beast howls for his blood. For vengeance."

"I think I understand," Kate said quietly. "At the very least, if we succeed tonight, you'll have the satisfaction of knowing that the pair who murdered your mother has been stopped. How they are stopped and what happens to them afterward is in the Goddess's hands."

"I guess I can live with that." Grif turned away from her then and spoke in a low voice to his brothers, no doubt issuing orders. Kate turned to Slade as he put his arm around her shoulders.

"We'll do what we can to stop her, but if it comes down to it, Grif deserves the kill." His bald statement really drove home to Kate the fact that she wasn't dealing with regular people here. These were shifters, with animal instincts only slightly tempered by their human sides. The animal wanted to kill, and she couldn't blame them for that.

"All right."

Kate's attention was caught by Steve, who was transforming back to his human shape. She'd seen him naked before, of course, but not all of him, standing there, twisting and flexing those impressive muscles as he re-dressed in his black commando gear. She saw him slip the earpiece into his ear with practiced ease. He also had a backpack in the truck, which he removed and began rummaging through.

Mean looking weapons began to appear and then disappear just as quickly once he'd checked them over and stashed them on his person. She had to hand it to him, he certainly knew how to disguise the fact that he was armed to the teeth.

Robert stayed in his animal form and Kate realized he didn't have the same military experience as Grif and Steve. He was probably stealthier—and deadlier—in his beast form. The older brothers though, they were equally dangerous on two legs or four.

So was Slade, for that matter. Of that, she had no doubt.

CHAPTER TWELVE

Only minutes later, Kate found herself walking side by side with Slade, wearing a hard hat and trying her best to unravel all the magical signatures left behind by a multitude of shifters. She couldn't illuminate the magic the way she'd done in the Redstone's backyard. No, that would be too obvious. The sorceress would see them coming a mile away.

Slade was tamping down his magic, dampening it in a way she hadn't known anyone could before she met him. They did a little experimentation and discovered that if she stayed close to him, he could extend his dampening field to include her too. That was handy.

The plan was to walk along the edges of the vast property. Slade had given her a clipboard and pen and from time to time they'd stop and Slade would gesture while she pretended to take notes. He'd taken on the role of site inspector with chameleon-like grace.

"Perimeter breach," Slade whispered as they walked. He must've heard it over the earpiece he still wore. "Moore's men on the southeast fence saw her come through. She was moving fast and went straight into the base of the structure. Damn." Slade switched on the mic and began relaying orders as they changed direction, heading for the north entrance to the steel skeleton of the building. "Get everyone out of there," Slade was saying in a low, urgent voice as they moved quickly toward their objective.

Even as they entered the building, Kate saw about fifteen workers exiting. They were evacuating, but making it look like they were just taking a break. Only a select few raptors would be left on the upper floors— enough to make it convincing, but none of them were pushovers. All were strong men with years of experience who had volunteered for this especially hazardous duty. They were part of Redstone's group. They'd known the matriarch, and wanted to help catch her killers.

"Block the exits and set up a perimeter around the building. Box her in," Slade said with finality as he stopped and scanned the lattice-like structure above their heads. Only a few floors had partial decking. Most of the place was still bare iron.

He turned off the mic, though she knew he could still hear as the team members reported over the radio. Kate was following his lead. They hadn't been able to discuss every contingency, but they had touched on a few different things they could try if they ended up inside the building with the sorceress, as had just happened.

Kate had really thought the woman would target her victim from outside, but she'd done the unexpected. Thankfully, Slade and the other guys seemed more than capable of adjusting for many different contingencies. Kate was glad now that they'd discussed more than just what she'd assumed would happen.

"What now?" Kate whispered to him as he continued to scan the heights.

"We need to pinpoint her location," he replied without looking at her. His keen blue eyes were trained on the steel above them. "We'll try this the stealthy way first, but if we can't find her in three minutes, we'll light the place up with magic."

"She'll know we're here," Kate objected, though on reflection she saw the need for urgency.

"She'll find that out sooner or later. I'm hoping for later, but we need to flush her out before she can launch her attack. I'd prefer to sneak up on her..." His voice trailed off as his gaze halted and searched one particular area.

"Do you see her?" Kate held her breath, nervous for his answer.

"I think..." Slade moved slightly, still concentrating on one spot, far above their heads. "Bingo."

He kept his eyes trained on the woman only he could see as he ran for the nearest elevator. Kate just barely kept up with him and jumped into the metal contraption a moment before it started moving a fast clip up the side of the steel girders. It was an open cage affair, strictly for use during construction. The much fancier, permanent passenger elevators had yet to be installed, though the shafts had already been framed out in several different parts of the structure.

"I have her in sight," Slade reported over the radio. "Nineteenth floor. South side. Closing in on the raptors from the floor below."

Kate looked as they rose higher and could just make out a darker shape against the shadows of the decking. The nineteenth floor had more of the flooring on the south side than some of the other parts of the building. They seemed to be using it as a staging area for materials that would be used as they constructed the upper floors and there were pallets of supplies and the dark silhouettes of equipment dotting the area.

Work lights illuminated the area, strung every ten feet or so. They put off a stark white light that left deep shadows. It was to the shadows that they clung as they got off the elevator the floor below, then made their way up one of the staircases to the nineteenth story.

Yellow caution tape fluttered in the night breeze, the only thing guarding the open sides of the building and the areas that had no decking. Kate had never been up in a building that wasn't even close to finished. Everything about the situation was scary—from the danger of plummeting to her death, to the idea of facing a cold-blooded murderer.

But Slade was with her. In the short time she'd known him, he'd become her lifeline. Her rock. The only man she had ever felt comfortable in leaning on when she needed a little boost, be it magical, emotional or physical. His presence gave her comfort and strength. She could face anything as long as he was by her side.

They were nearing the woman when Kate felt something very wrong. Very dark. Evil.

"She's doing something," Kate warned Slade in the barest whisper she could manage. The noise from machinery and the night wind would make it hard for human hearing to pick up the noise of their approach or any whispering they might need to do, but Slade would hear a lot more with his sharp, shifter senses.

"I feel it too," he confirmed. He had positioned them behind a relatively large generator that was about fifteen yards away from the woman. The generator was off and the shadows it cast hid them well. "Get ready. I want you to light up all the magic here like you did in the backyard and I want you to do it before she has a chance to strike."

Kate didn't question why he wanted her to use something that wasn't offensive at all. He had his reasons. If nothing else, suddenly seeing all the magic around her in bright, brilliant color would startle the woman.

Kate nodded at him. "I'm ready when you are."

"That's my girl." Slade winked at her, sparing her a hint of a smile. She realized that he was actually enjoying himself—just the tiniest bit—but he clearly liked this kind of work. And why not? He seemed perfectly suited for it.

He spoke quietly into the radio and Kate felt the building of energy. The sorceress was preparing her spell. "Slade..." she whispered, nervous.

"Okay, kitten. Do it now."

Kate let loose with her own power and the entire place lit up with magic. Bright, beautiful, shifter magic. And one, disgusting trail of blood red, leading to the place where the sorceress hid. She was fully illuminated to Kate's senses now—Slade's too, she was sure.

Kate kept her magic going full force while Slade stepped into the open, drawing the woman's attention.

"It's over," he said in a strong voice that carried. "You're caught. Might as well give up now, Sheila."

She jumped at the sound of her name, but otherwise made no reply. Kate felt the dark power ratchet up a moment before the sorceress lobbed a magical fireball at Slade. He shifted shape in the blink of an eye and when Kate's vision cleared from the intensity of the magic thrown their way, Slade wasn't in his black leopard form. No, he wore a glowing, spotted white coat and his paws and tail were incredibly bushy.

"You've got to be kidding me. He's a snow leopard?"

Even Kate had heard the rumors—the myths, really. Rarer than rare, snow leopards were like shifter royalty or something. And intensely magical.

That part was proving true as the sorceress's energy seemed to bounce right off him. Amazing.

Even as she watched, Slade leapt. He covered a huge distance in a single bound and kept going...climbing and dancing along the steel girders and decking toward the fleeing mage.

Kate kept her magic going strong, illuminating the scene as best she could for Slade. To the others it probably looked like she was simply hiding behind the generator, but to those with magesight, the sorceress's path was lit with bright, blood red light against the purer colors of the shifter's magic—and the pure blue and white streak of Slade's alternate form.

Or his *other* alternate form. Was it even possible for one shifter to claim two different animal forms? Kate had never heard of such a thing, but then again, she'd never met a snow leopard before either. Nobody had. Not to her knowledge.

It seemed there was a first time for everything.

She tried to watch Slade's progress as he chased the sorceress but he was faster than her eyes could follow. So was the sorceress. She was augmenting her speed with magic in order to stay one step ahead of Slade—and the cougars who had joined the chase.

Four of the Redstone brothers had joined the fray, ducking the magical attacks of the sorceress by sheer skill and agility while Slade barreled right through them as if they were nothing. In fact those fireballs were enough to kill most other shifters. Or at least knock them off their feet. Or off the side of the building.

Kate saw a series of giant hawks and eagles diving from the upper floors, getting out of the way while the cats ran the mage to ground. Kate kept a tight hold on her concentration, not allowing the magic to flare too brightly while keeping it illuminated to help Slade track the woman.

She saw the way he directed and worked with the other cats. The cougars were clearly angry. Hell, they were irate. But Slade managed to exert his influence on them, even as he led the small group in a concerted effort to trap the woman between them.

She fled around all the obstacles piled on the deck, faster than Kate would have believed if she hadn't seen it herself. But the cats were faster. The sorceress threw sickly blood-red fireballs at them, but none made contact. Slade kept himself the main focus of her attacks as best he could, but she took shots at the cougars too.

Until they cornered her. She was stuck between three long pallets of decking material on one side, the cougars on the other, Slade in front and the sheer drop off the side of the building behind her.

Slade shifted back to his human form, fully clothed and facing the sorceress. Kate moved, holding her magic at the ready.

"Give up, Sheila. You're done," Slade said with finality.

"Do I know you?" she asked and her voice was low and sultry, magical.

She was trying to exert seductive magic over the men but Kate saw it and intercepted it, illuminating its oozing crimson for Slade to see. Slade nodded and raised one hand, pushing the magic back at her, disdain clear on his face that seemed to anger the sorceress.

"I know all about you, Sheila. I know you went rogue on your masters in the *Venifucus*. I know your pal Abrahamson has betrayed you. He gave me the chalice you meant to use for your little ceremony and I destroyed it." Slade advanced on the woman as if she was no threat to him.

And perhaps she wasn't. Slade had seemed to take the full brunt of her magical fireballs with impunity.

He took a little poetic license with the facts about the chalice, but Kate wouldn't quibble. Especially not when she saw how mad the thought of losing the chalice made the other woman.

"You couldn't have. I'd know," Sheila sneered.

"Would you?" Slade advanced even closer, one eyebrow raised mockingly. "You didn't even know when I captured Abrahamson."

191

Her eyes widened. She hadn't known, Kate realized. So maybe this woman wasn't as powerful as they'd thought. Kate wouldn't drop her guard though. That would be a foolish mistake.

"He is nothing," the sorceress spat. "As you are nothing. I will reveal your existence to the human world and they will hunt you all."

"Really?" Slade crossed his arms. "And how do you propose to do that? You're surrounded. You can't escape."

"Can't I?" She smiled and looked sharply over her shoulder.

Kate gasped. Did she intend to jump? It sure looked like it to Kate.

But then an enormous, cream colored owl landed on the open side of the building. To Kate's magesight, the owl was lit with intense magic. More than any other shifter she'd seen...except Slade.

The woman threw her magic at the giant owl, but it bounced off. Just bounced. Kate didn't have any other way to describe what happened. It wasn't like the way Slade had charged through the fireballs that had been lobbed at him. This was an actual bounce.

The sorceress jumped when her magic was repelled back at her. She jumped higher than Kate would have credited, up and over the pallet of decking material at her side.

The cougars bounded on top of the stacks of decking as the woman screamed. Then the scream cut off abruptly and Kate heard a distant thud.

Oh, no.

Slade was around the pallets like a shot, but he stopped short, swaying slightly as Kate rounded the oversized pallets and realized what had happened. There was an open, unfinished elevator shaft just behind the pallets.

Slade held her back when Kate would have looked down the shaft. He had his arm around her waist and curled her into his chest, protectively.

"Do you think she realized the shaft was there?" Kate whispered as the cougars took off, bounding away to get to the bottom of the shaft in a much safer manner.

They took the stairs, which were right next to the open shaft. Only the owl remained, perched now on the side of the elevator shaft, watching with icy gray eyes.

"No, kitten. She would have used her magic to break her fall if she'd been prepared for it. I believe she had the capability, which was why she was going to go over the side. But our new friend Johan here blocked her retreat." Slade gestured toward the giant owl. "Thank you, Johan."

The owl hooted once, then hopped away, taking to the air when he reached the open side of the building. Kate watched his creamy wings. He had to have a six foot wingspan at the very least.

Kate couldn't feel the malevolent energy of the sorceress anymore. It had dissipated.

"Is she dead?" Kate asked quietly, unable and really, unwilling at the moment, to look down the empty shaft.

"Yeah, I think so. Grif will verify, as is his right. He's going to have to be content with running her to ground. She caused her own death. Her blood is on her own hands."

"I think that's better for all concerned. I know you shifters take killing as a natural part of your existence, but this kind of thing..." She searched for words to describe what she felt in her heart. "A revenge killing, motivated by anger and hate..." She turned in Slade's arms and looked up into his beautiful blue eyes. "It injures the soul. I wouldn't want that for Grif or any of his brothers."

"You are wise beyond your years, my love," Slade whispered before leaning down to place a gentle kiss on her lips.

She wanted more, but he moved away, though he kept his arm around her waist. He ushered them both back from the edge of the shaft after taking one last look over the edge. Kate resisted. She didn't want to see what had become of the evil woman. It couldn't be pretty. Falling nineteen stories had to have done serious damage.

A little thrill went through her as she realized what Slade had called her. *His love*. Wouldn't it be amazing if she really were his love? She wanted it so much, but knew it was probably only an impossible daydream.

Arm in arm, they walked back to the elevator. Slade was solicitous of her in a way that made her feel special and cared for. It was a nice feeling. Even after he closed the cage door of the construction elevator and the rig started to trundle down to the ground, he pulled her into his arms and just held her, in silence, all the way down.

When the door opened on the ground floor, he ushered her out and would have steered her away from the area where the cougars were gathered, but she stopped him. She needed to make sure the sorceress hadn't left any traces of her evil behind.

"Are you sure?" Slade asked when she turned toward the direction of the elevator shaft. "It's not pretty."

"I've seen death before," she answered. "And it's my duty to protect the Redstone Clan and be certain any magical residue is channeled away from where it could cause harm. I have to check." She really didn't want to, but knew she had a duty to perform. She had to suck it up and do her job.

Slade looked at her for a moment and she thought she saw respect in his eyes. She knew then, she'd chosen the right path. It had been tempting to chicken out and let him lead her away from the undoubtedly gruesome sight, but she had a responsibility to the Redstones, to the shifters who worked for them, and even to the people who would one day use this building, when it was finished.

Slade was impressed by the way Kate carried herself over to the milling cougars. She walked among them with no fear, even as they growled in frustration. The cats had not had the pleasure of the kill, though satisfaction was clear in the set of their shoulders. Grif quieted his brothers the moment the Kate stepped through the circle of cougars prowling around the body.

The Alpha sat back on his haunches and that simple act brought his brothers to his side. They all sat, facing Kate and the dead sorceress, watching attentively. Slade was impressed as Kate acted in her role as priestess, sending out her magic one more time to do battle with the residue of evil that surrounded the fallen mage.

It was no contest. Slade could see that easily with his magesight as the pure Light of the Lady worked through Kate once again to negate and consign what was left of the sorceress's magic to the cleansing depths of the earth.

Grif stood as witness, the clear leader. Steve, Robert, and Matt sat at their elder brother's side. Mag hadn't been seen since taking the vampire away from Abrahamson's house, though he had called to say he was all right. Still, the majority of the Redstone family was present to witness the passing of the woman who had killed their mother.

Kate said ritual words and worked her magic, ensuring the mage's evil power and intent would never cause anyone harm again. Slade watched, as did the cougars. More people joined the circle around the open elevator shaft as Kate's Goddess-given magic lit the scene to Slade's magesight.

Slade was unsurprised to find Johan at his side. The owl shifter had arrived on silent, human feet, but Slade had felt his intensely magical presence. He remained silent as he watched Kate with a speculative look to his face that Slade found intriguing.

When the ritual concluded, the men of the Ghost Squad were all present, standing respectfully and with care for Kate's safety. Even when the enemy had been dealt with, these men were still on guard. As it should be. Their life was vigilance. As Slade's had been until very recently.

Oh, he would never lose the habit, but he'd found something else to focus on in the past few days. Or, rather, some*one* else. Kate had proven herself in every way, to the point that Slade knew she was too good for him, but still, he was going to try with all his might to win her heart.

The time had come to claim his mate.

Kate finished the ceremony, but didn't leave the fallen woman's side. She bent and picked up the woman's large purse. It looked very plain at first glance, but once the evil magic of the mage had been banished, the designer leather bag shone with a subtle, magical light to Slade's eyes.

Kate looked up at him just for a moment before opening the bag as if seeking strength. He liked that she would turn to him, even unconsciously for reassurance. She peered inside the bag and then shut her eyes in what looked like a mix of relief and sorrow. She closed the bag and walked up to the Alpha cougar at a respectful pace.

"What was taken from your mother is now returned," Kate said in a solemn tone. "With your permission, I will return this to the matriarch, so we can send her off to the next world in peace."

Grif bowed his head and his brothers followed suit as Kate moved between them, carrying her precious burden. She walked straight to Slade's side, holding tight to the leather bag as he escorted her out of the building.

The Ghost Squad melted into the night, watching their path and clearing any obstacles to the garage. Grif and his brothers bounded ahead through the shadows, entering the garage through the hidden door.

By the time Slade and Kate had made it across the site and into the structure, all four cougars were men once again, dressed and waiting for them with solemn expressions. They said not a word as Slade seated Kate in his rented vehicle. She kept the leather bag on her lap.

Steve stopped at the passenger door to look in at Kate. She rolled down the window and Slade pretended not to notice the tears in the cougar's golden eyes.

"Thank you," Steve said in a raspy tone. "It didn't turn out like I expected, but I think justice has been served." He cleared his throat, looking away for a moment as he gathered himself. "Having you here has helped the Clan, Kate. Grif will say the same. But I wanted to tell you what he probably won't say. Your presence here has brought some measure of peace to our family." Steve seemed to grow stronger as he said the words. Grif and Robert were piling into their truck, waiting on Steve, but he took his time to say the words that seemed so important to him.

"I'm glad," Kate said simply. "Thanks for saying that. It's not only my duty, but my honor to help."

Steve nodded once, slapped his open palm against the saddle of the open window, and left, walking straighter, gaining strength as Slade and Kate watched after him. Kate rolled up the window and Slade put the SUV in gear.

Steve got into the truck with Grif and Robert while Matt straddled the motorcycle that had appeared in the garage since they'd first arrived. He'd been late to the party, but he'd been there at the crucial moment.

"You did good, kitten," Slade said quietly as they rolled out of the garage.

"I don't ever want to be involved in something this dark again if I can help it, but I'm glad I was able to help."

"None of us ever *want* to face evil, but it's out there. Those of us who are put in a position to fight it just do the best we can. And sweetheart, you did us all proud with your fierceness tempered by compassion. You've enriched this shifter community just by your presence. That's what Steve was trying to say. You're good for them and now they all know it in the most direct terms." Slade tried to give her something positive to focus on. She seemed so forlorn, he wanted to reach out and comfort her, but he had to drive.

"Take us home, Slade," she said quietly. "It's time the matriarch was put to rest."

Kate didn't speak again until they arrived back at the Redstone homestead, but Slade held her hand when he saw the tears rolling silently down her cheeks.

They made a small convoy of vehicles heading back to the housing development. Slade and Kate followed Matt on the motorcycle, riding point. Grif's truck followed them, and in turn was followed by a number of other vehicles. All found spots on the street outside the Redstone's home and even Slade was surprised to see the members of the Ghost Squad, including their mysterious owl-shifter healer, had come to pay their final respects to the Redstone matriarch.

Slade realized as he watched the soldiers each spend a few moments talking to Grif and Steve, that many of them were former comrades-in-arms. They would stand with their friends during their time of grief. Such was the shifter way. Moreover, such was the code of the soldiers they would always be, even though Grif had retired to be Alpha of his Clan and leader of an even larger collection of shifter construction workers and their families.

Kate went into the house with the bag held tightly in her hands. When Slade offered to help, she smiled softly at him and demurred. It was her responsibility as priestess to prepare the mother of the Clan for her final journey.

So Slade stayed outside, joining the gathering in the big backyard, in the garden the older lady had so lovingly tended. It was a fitting place for her final ritual. A good place for her children to say goodbye and share their grief with their friends.

"You're snowcat." The tone of the older man's voice wasn't exactly accusatory. Johan, the owl shifter, had walked silently to Slade's side and spoke in a soft voice that didn't carry beyond the two of them.

"Only half," Slade confirmed. There wasn't much point in denying his heritage now. Everyone at the construction site had probably seen his glowing white alternate form. There was really no hiding the snowcat when he let him out.

"Less than half, if I don't miss my guess, but the snowcat breeds true. How far back was your snowcat ancestor?" The owl seemed to know a lot more than Slade was comfortable with, but this Johan had something very mystical about him. He was also a rare kind of shifter and Slade had never seen such an impressive owl among the few he'd met in his travels.

"My great-grandmother."

"She must be very proud of you." Johan nodded as he spoke.

That was interesting. Most people would have assumed his great-grandmother was long dead, but the owl seemed to know more about snowcats than Slade had realized. Then again, owls were noted for their wisdom and knowledge. Maybe those stories about them being the guardians of shifter knowledge had a little bit of truth in them after all.

"I hope so," Slade answered noncommittally.

"You are unique among the snowcats I have known," Johan observed. "Most cannot hide their nature behind another form. I have never heard of the snowcat sharing space with a leopard. But the two beasts of your nature seem to have come to some kind of accord within your soul. You are blessed, indeed."

Slade didn't really know what to say to that, so he went with vaguely inquisitive. "Have you known many snowcats?"

"I have been to Tibet and flew the sacred mountain," Johan admitted with some pride in his voice.

Slade was impressed. He had never been to the secret snowcat enclave in the Himalayas, but it was a pilgrimage he wanted to make someday.

"What kind of owl are you? I admit, I have never seen your equal, Johan."

Johan smiled and his gray eyes twinkled. "We are called Eurasian Eagle-Owls by humans, but we prefer the term *hibou*."

"That's just the French word for owl," Slade observed.

Johan smiled. "That may be, but it goes farther back than the modern French. We've inhabited the continents on the other side of the world for centuries. And your great-grandmother's people have long been our allies, though they retreated into those mountains a long, long time ago. It wasn't as easy for those who are ground-bound to weather all the wars fought in those places among wizards, shifters, humans and anyone else who wanted to start trouble with their neighbors."

Slade thought about that for a moment and realized all that had happened in Asia, Europe and all the lands in between over the centuries. There were still volatile areas, even today, that saw more than their share of violence and war. It would not be easy for shifters — especially the meditative, mystical snowcats — to deal with that kind of upheaval going on all around them.

"So what brought you to Nevada, Johan. I get the impression that you came along to do a bit more than observe."

"Observation is but one of my callings, young man. And I have observed a very powerful priestess forming bonds with a surprising snowcat-leopard hybrid the likes of which I have never known. It is something to ponder, don't you agree?"

Slade didn't like knowing that he and Kate had somehow become a focus of this mysterious shifter's attention. Owls were crafty. The few he'd known over the years had always been at least two steps ahead of him in any plan he had devised. They were deep thinkers with deadly instincts tempered by unexpected compassion.

All in all, he'd liked those owls he'd known very much and found their friendship both stimulating and fulfilling. But this mysterious *hibou* was something else again. Slade didn't quite know what to make of him.

"What's between Kate and I is private, Johan." Slade met the man's gaze with a clear message in his own expression. He voice was firm and his stance strong. It would not do to show weakness to a predator of Johan's ability.

"Not for long," Johan said with an easy smile. "But I respect the fact that this is new and you have yet to declare yourself in terms her human mind can comprehend. Son..." Johan put one hand on Slade's arm in a comforting, almost fatherly way. "You need to spell it out for her. Soon. She was raised human. She does not understand shifter ways for all that she has chosen to live among us. She is uncertain of your commitment and it is up to you to make her feel secure." Johan removed his hand while Slade took in his words. "Please forgive an old man for offering advice where none was sought. I have seen too many youngsters make a hash of their early days together by not speaking clearly and I admit, I have a special interest in the young priestess. I want her to be happy."

Now wasn't that interesting?

"Why? What is she to you, Johan?" Slade's heart thundered in his ears. Something was strange here. He didn't think the owl was a threat to Kate, but there was definitely something amiss and Slade wanted to know what it was. Anything that related to Kate was his business — whether she realized it yet or not.

"All in good time, young snowcat. Have no fear for your mate's safety. What I know will bring comfort, if not outright joy, to her. But it is not yet time for the talk we must have. I will stay until that time comes."

The owl was right on one point. Slade had done a bad job of explaining what Kate meant to him. He wanted her as his mate. Forever.

Only he was scared she might reject him. That fear—as odd as that feeling was to him—was what had held him back from making the declarations he needed to make. He would remedy that as soon as possible, but at the moment they all had duties to attend.

Grif came out of the house with a young girl at his side. It must be Belinda, Slade realized, the youngest child of the matriarch. She wasn't even in her teens and her face was pale, eyes sad and filled with a lost expression. Of them all, little Belinda would probably have it toughest. She'd lost her older sister to violence just a short while ago and now had lost her mother in a horrific way. Her brothers would have to help the child and guide her as she grew. They'd have to protect her too.

So much tragedy in one family, Slade thought. And too much for such a young girl to deal with easily. Slade sent a prayer skyward for the girl and her brothers. It would be hard for them now, but he prayed they would all come through this terrible ordeal in time, with the Lady's help.

Friends began to arrive, the shifter community coming out in support of the Redstones. Even their giant backyard began to overflow with people and creatures, but there was no chaos. It was very orderly and solemn as each member of the Clan, and many of the employees of Redstone Construction and their family members, came over to pay their respects in low-voiced murmurs of condolence and heartfelt hugs. Silence fell when the back patio doors opened. Kate appeared and called the brothers inside. A moment later, they exited the house, carrying their mother's body on an ornate board between them. It had handholds carved into its surface and it was clear this ceremonial board had a long history of use in this Clan.

They proceeded solemnly until they reached the space that had been cleared for them. They lay the board amidst a flowerbed that was rife with color and life. The matriarch lay upon it, her hands folded, her dress colorful and bright, her eyes closed and her lifeless body looking as beautiful as she always had throughout her life.

Shifters did not bury their dead the way humans did. In fact, unless a priestess intervened, their bodies usually faded away into energy within a day or two of death, leaving no trace behind of their existence. That was just part of why they had been able to hide their existence from the rest of the world for so very long.

Kate had done her work here, allowing time for them to recover the piece of pelt that had been carved away. Once returned, Slade assumed the matriarch had reverted to her human form. Kate had cared for her body, dressing her in a favorite outfit with loving care and laying her out on the ritual board of the Clan.

The matriarch would have a proper sendoff. Kate had seen to that.

Everyone gathered around and Kate began the ceremony that would release her body and soul to the earth and stars. Slade felt the magic build and knew the moment Kate let go of her hold on the magic.

The body crystallized into a million points of light, half heading for the heavens and half sinking into the earth, through the carved wooden board, into the flowerbed and the rich soil beneath. It was a solemn moment and Slade heard the soft sobbing of the young girl. It broke his heart to think of her loss, but he knew he'd done all he could to bring justice.

It would never bring her mother back, but he hoped, in time, it would bring peace to her troubled heart.

CHAPTER THIRTEEN

Slade stood back, watching as Kate performed her duties and then paused to comfort the child. The shifters were speaking in low tones, most offering touches of sympathy to the Alpha and his family. They moved away toward the house, leaving the backyard and the minimal cleanup to the priestess.

Kate knelt by the burial board and used her magic to inscribe one more name on it. That of the matriarch. All the other names that covered its surface had been carved the old fashioned way, Slade saw. He stood over her shoulder, offering silent comfort.

The letters Kate carved with her magic were lovely and ornate—almost vine-like.

"She would like this," Kate said, sniffing a little as emotion overtook her. "She loved her garden and growing things. Almost as much as she loved her children."

"She was a good mother, from all accounts. To more than just her family. The Clan will miss her." Slade knelt at Kate's side and put his arm around her trembling shoulders.

"I'll miss her too. She was instrumental in making me welcome here. As soon as she accepted me, everyone else began to warm to me." Kate leaned her head against Slade's shoulder. He loved being the one she would turn to when she needed to lean on someone. If he had his way, she would do so for the rest of their lives.

They stayed like that for a long moment, letting the night sounds deepen. The backyard was almost empty now, except for a few stragglers who were on their way either into the Redstone house or off to their own places.

Slowly, Kate straightened and began folding the clothing that had not transformed into energy along with the matriarch's body. "The family will want these," she said idly as she made a neat pile of them. "They were among her favorites. This skirt is by a designer she favored and I know for a fact she loved the colors. Just looking at it brings back good memories of the first time I met her."

Kate sobbed and turned to Slade. He took her in his arms as she finally gave in to her grief. She had been so strong and vigilant in her pursuit of the killers. She'd kept her own grief bottled tightly inside while they needed her to focus on the trail.

Now that things had been settled, she was finally free to cry for the woman she would miss. And Slade was there to hold her as she shook with sadness and her tears stained his shirt. He would be nowhere else but here at this moment, offering comfort when his mate needed him.

That's what mates did. They helped each other and were there for each other in good times and bad. They shared joy and sadness...and whatever else came their way.

He would do that for Kate. Gladly.

For the rest of their lives.

They sat there together, on the lush green grass of the Redstone's backyard, the silence of the night surrounding them as everyone left them alone at the resting place of the much beloved matriarch. Nobody intruded on Kate's grief. They seemed to understand. And those few who paused to look at her on their way out of the yard seemed to smile softly at the picture she and Slade must've made—the strong Alpha cat letting the frail human priestess lean on him when her own emotional strength gave out.

She hadn't meant to collapse this way. She wasn't usually much of a crier. But these past few days had been rough on everyone. Everything that had happened since she had felt that unmistakable surge of evil as she'd tried to greet the sun had affected her deeply.

The evil magic. The devastating discovery of the matriarch's body. The desperate hunt for her killers and the confrontations with both mages. All of that had taken something out of her. Only Slade's steady presence at her side—and in her bed last night—had seen her through such dire circumstances.

She would have been lost to her grief long before now if she hadn't had him to lean on. She needed him. And wanted him in her life forever. Not just for today.

Kate straightened up, putting space between them as she wiped at her eyes. She had to get control over her wayward emotions.

"Sorry," she whispered, not looking at Slade. "I never fall apart like this."

"You're entitled." He was so kind, though she bet he didn't often have weeping women slobbering all over him. Most men ran from the sight of women's tears. "You've had a rough couple of days."

"So have you," she countered. "And you're not crying."

"I'm crying on the inside," he answered, shocking her gaze up to meet his. There was only a small twinkle in his hypnotic blue eyes. He was serious. At least in part. He made her smile, even through her tears.

"You're a heck of a guy, Slade." She had to marvel at his resilience, his strength, his magic. Which reminded her… "And a snow leopard? But I saw your black leopard form and it looked different. Is that even possible?"

"We call them snowcats and my great-grandmother is one. The other side of my heritage is the black leopard you saw first, but in me, something is a little different than in most mixed-heritage shifters. I have both the snowcat and the leopard in my soul. Somehow, they get along. But I don't let the snowcat out often. Other shifters tend to react strangely to it."

"Snowcats are holy men, I've heard. Tibetan mystics. They're revered among shifters, aren't they?" She was feeling steadier as their conversation helped distract her from her grief. She loved learning about shifters — especially Slade, in particular.

"Yeah," he sighed. "It can get a little difficult sometimes. They seem to expect me to know all the secrets of the universe and I'm more a man of action than contemplation."

"The snowcat must be part of you for a reason," she insisted, not quite knowing where the wisdom was coming from, but it felt right. Sometimes it happened that way. She knew things without knowing how she knew them.

"If you say so. Personally, I think it's the magic that attracted it. I was born with more magic than most of my family, though a few of them are snowcats too. The snowcat tends to show up a few times in each generation of my family, but there's more than one like me—with both snowcat and leopard. We're a little different than most shifters."

"You can say that again." She smiled as she rested her head lightly on his shoulder. They were still in each other's arms, sitting on the grass, the night wind blowing softly against her cheek. "You're a very special man, Slade."

"I hope you mean that." Suddenly there was a new intensity in his voice that made her look up into his eyes, so close to her own.

"Why?" Her voice was the breath of a whisper in the stillness of the night. It was as if the whole world paused to watch what might happen in the next few moments.

"I love you, Kate. I want you to be with me always. You are my mate."

Kate didn't hear much beyond his first three words. So simple. So life-altering. A smile blossomed out from within and tears started forming behind her eyes again. Happy tears this time.

"I love you too."

The intense blue of his eyes flared even higher as her softly spoken words seemed to penetrate.

"You do? So soon? I thought it took longer for humans to decide such things."

"Maybe it does, but I think I fell in love with you the moment we met," she admitted shyly.

"Me too," he agreed with both enthusiasm and joyful laughter. "I thought that only happened to shifters. I know I've never felt this way before. And I never will feel like this about any other female. You're the only one for me, Kate, if you'll have me."

"If? Oh, Slade, there's no question. I'm yours if you want me."

"No *ifs* on my side either, my dearest love." His arms tightened around her as his head lowered. "I love you for all time," he breathed, his lips against hers before he claimed her in the first kiss of the rest of their lives.

Kate wasn't sure how they got back to her place. She remembered holding hands as they walked to the curb and then a short drive and then...delicious chaos as Slade lifted her off her feet and carried her not only into her home, but up the stairs and straight into her bedroom.

He looked around approvingly before placing her on the queen sized bed. "I like the décor in here better."

"What? You don't enjoy grandma flowers for everyday living?" She laughed with him as they both began to take off their clothes.

"While *my* grandma—and *great*-grandma—will love it, I'm sure, I prefer something a little more modern. I like what you've done here. It looks green and growing. Feminine but not overpoweringly so."

She was surprised and pleased by his comments. She'd chosen the dark green design out of all the ones she'd seen at the store because the green vines with the occasional small blue flowers attracted her eye from the first moment she'd seen it. The print coordinated with dark, forest green sheets and blue accent pillows and furniture. The walls were a neutral cream color, trimmed with dashes of periwinkle and deeper blue here and there.

She loved the way the room had come out and enjoyed her personal sanctuary. It made her happy to think Slade liked it too.

"Wait. Did you say your great-grandmother?"

"Yep." Slade shrugged out of his shirt and came over to sit on the bed beside her, drawing her close. "She taught me everything I learned about magic before I was twelve. I know she'll come running the moment she learns I've finally found my mate. Be prepared. The entire Clan will descend upon us if I don't take you home for a visit at the earliest opportunity."

"Really?" Kate felt her heart fill with both hope and fear. She'd never had a family before. The prospect was both amazing and daunting. "Do you think they'll like me? I mean, I'm not a shifter."

Slade lowered his head to kiss her lips once, very gently. "They will love you because you're the only woman in the world who can complete me. They will love your kind heart and gentle ways. Your fierce courage and Goddess-given magic. How could they not, when I love you with all my being? They'll see what I see when I look at you." He kissed her again, this time with more passion. "They will see a bright and loving future for not only us, but for the Clan. Great-grandmother will especially love the fact that you are a priestess."

"I hope you're right." She bit her lip nervously, but Slade kissed her again, taking her lip between his own teeth for a quick, painless nip before letting her go again.

"Trust me, kitten. I know them as well as I know myself. Eventually, you will too. Snowcats live a very long time. You'll have centuries to get used to them."

"Centuries?" She pushed against his shoulders, needing to check that she'd heard him correctly.

Slade smiled at her. "Yeah." He looked a little chagrinned. "It's not widely known, but all that magic snowcats have…well, it brings with it a few perks. One of them is a longer life span for us and most of the time, for our chosen mates as well. I can already feel the way our magics are joining and twining, can't you?"

"I—" She'd noticed the meshing of their magics, but hadn't quite known what it could mean. The very idea of what he was suggesting boggled her mind.

"It's okay. We have the rest of our lives to figure it out." He kissed her again and pushed her back on the soft bed, coming over her to block out the soft glow of the light fixture on the ceiling.

He made love to her slowly. Gently demonstrating his love for her in the most sensuous way possible. He brought her to climax twice before joining her in bliss, then did it all over again.

Predictably, after the tumult of the night before, Slade and Kate slept in the next morning. They had just enjoyed a leisurely climax or two and were starting to make brunch in the kitchen downstairs when the doorbell rang.

Slade was flipping pancakes when Kate went to answer the door. He could hear the surprise in her voice as she welcomed the old owl into her home. He reintroduced himself and she invited him to join them in some refreshment, guiding him into the kitchen, which was at the back of the house. Slade added more batter to the griddle and turned to say hello as they entered the room.

"Good to see you again, Johan." Slade held out his hand for a quick shake.

The owl's gray eyes twinkled, taking in the domestic scene. "Likewise," he answered shortly.

Kate invited him to sit at the kitchen table as Slade served up breakfast. They held off any serious topics of conversation until after they'd eaten the majority of the pile of pancakes and mound of bacon he'd prepared, for which Slade was grateful. He suspected whatever the strange shifter had to say, it would be significant.

"So what brings you here this morning?" Slade finally asked as he downed the last of his pancakes. Kate had finished eating long before the men, and was attentive as she sipped her coffee.

"It is a matter of solving a mystery and bringing news that I hope will be happy." The owl was as inscrutable as his animal counterpart. "Katherine, what do you know of your birth parents?"

Kate sat up straight in her chair, clearly caught off guard by the question.

"Nothing, really. They died in an accident and I was given to a foster family to raise. It didn't really work out. The first family was trying to adopt because they'd thought they couldn't have children of their own, but then the woman got pregnant about two years after taking me in. I was only about three or four when I went to a second family. I stayed with them for a few years before Mr. Samuels died and his wife realized she couldn't afford to keep me. I went to live with the Baxters next, then the Jeffersons until I turned eighteen. They were nice and we still keep in touch from time to time, but they raised about twenty different kids over the years and they don't know anything about my religious beliefs. They are fundamentalists and I'd rather not upset them." She looked down and away as if ashamed of her lack of any real connection to a parental figure.

Johan sighed. "I'm sorry, child. I had no idea until recently how tough you had it. To my shame, I had no idea until a few weeks ago that you even existed. You see, my daughter, Renee, married a mage named Albert. The Clan did not like Albert and felt he had only married Renee in order to gain our knowledge. I will never be certain of the truth of that, but I do have my suspicions." Johan's gray eyes narrowed, then his expression softened. "Regardless, Renee loved the mage and they ran away together to America. At the time, we were living in Breda. That's in the Netherlands."

Kate was intrigued by his story, but didn't really see what it had to do with her, unless...

"About five years ago, we decided to come to America and see if we could reestablish communication with Renee. I found out recently that both Renee and Albert had died in an accident more than two dozen years ago." His expression was one of deep sorrow. "I never got to reconcile with my girl and that I will always regret."

Kate reached out to the older man, putting one hand over his on the table, offering comfort. "You will see her again, one day, and both of your spirits will rejoice." Of that she had no doubt.

Johan turned his hand over and clasped hers tightly. "Until that time, I would like to make peace with you, Katherine. For I have little doubt, you are the daughter of Renee and Albert. You are my granddaughter."

Kate was floored by his declaration, but she felt the truth of it as her magic reached out and recognized his. Their magic was alike in some ways—those subtle ways she had never been able to articulate to her priestess teachers, who had all been human.

She felt tears gather in her eyes to answer the matching wetness she saw in Johan's gray eyes.

"I—" She had to pause to swallow her emotion. "I feel the truth of your words, but forgive me, I'm kind of astounded. I've never had any family before."

"You do now, if you wish to claim us. You are a member of the Hager Clan of *hibou* shifters." Johan spoke in softly accented English. His accent seemed to grow stronger when he was more emotional.

"So I have shifter blood after all?" Somehow that idea made her feel so much better about being with Slade. She wasn't just a weak human with a little magic. She was part shifter too. Wouldn't that make her more acceptable to his Clan?

But now she had a Clan of her own. Goddess be praised. This was turning out to be one of the happiest days of her life. Coming on the heels of such tragedy and one of the scariest things she'd ever participated in, this was like some huge reward — not only a life mate, but a long-lost family too?

"You are half *hibou* and half mage. You come by your magic from both sides of your heritage."

"I can't shift," she stated baldly. He had to realize she wasn't a shifter.

"That doesn't make you any less my granddaughter. I'm sorry it took me so long to realize it. You would have been raised among your cousins and the rest of the Clan if we had known you were out there."

"It's okay." She tried to comfort the older man who seemed to feel real distress over her past. "The Goddess works in mysterious ways."

They spent an hour or two talking about the Hager Clan and Kate's place in it. Slade kept mostly silent, but he was happy for his new mate. She'd had a rough start to life but if he had anything to say about it, her future would be as happy as he could make it. Finding her family was just the first step. Joining his Clan would come in time and he knew his relatives would make her feel welcome.

Slade left them talking in the kitchen for a few minutes to make some calls. He had to begin the process of moving. He'd come to the conclusion that it would be much easier for him to join Kate here in Nevada than to ask her to give up her place with the Redstones and join him in Montana.

He didn't really have much to offer her there anyway. He'd prowled from place to place for decades and hadn't had a real home since he'd left his family so long ago. Leaving his position with the Lords was a small price to pay to be with his mate. He was sure Tim and Rafe would understand.

Slade called them first. As the highest ranking *weres* on the continent, they were the right place to start the ball rolling. He'd then go talk to Grif, if the Alpha would see him. Slade was sure the family would be sticking close together today. He didn't want to intrude on their grief, but he wanted to ask Grif if he'd allow Slade to move into the neighborhood.

It was up to Grif, as Alpha, to grant Slade the right to live among his Clan or not. And Slade thought maybe he'd be able to offer some comfort to the Alpha. Being around Kate was rubbing off. His great-grandmother had always told him he'd embrace his snowcat heritage more fully when he found his mate. He hadn't believed her, but now that his dual nature had been seen, the snowcat was bound to cause a shift in attitude.

He welcomed it...now. Though Slade had spent most of his life as a man of action, he found the idea of cultivating his compassionate side—in Kate's company—was becoming more appealing.

Slade called the Redstone house and wasn't surprised when Valerie answered.

"I'm glad you called," she said, preempting his words.

"What can I do for you?"

"Grif wants to see you," she replied quickly. "Can you come over for lunch? It'll be quiet, but I'm making sure everyone eats."

"Kate too?" Slade didn't want to leave her alone. He wanted her around him constantly now.

"Sure. Bring her along," Valerie said easily. "We'll see you around one?"

"We'll be there," Slade confirmed. "Thanks."

A half hour later, Johan had gone with the promise to return for dinner. He was calling his Clan and plans were being made to get together. Slade knew Kate was apprehensive about meeting her kin, but Johan had no doubts. He was open about wanting to bring her into the Clan she should have been part of all her life.

Regardless of how it worked out—whether Kate wanted to go visit them, or they came here to see her—Slade would be by her side throughout. She would not face this alone, but he privately thought she had little to worry about. If Johan was any indication, she would be welcomed with open arms by her mother's people.

Slade and Kate walked to the Alpha's home, only a few blocks away along the winding streets of the development. They had a little time to kill before the lunch appointment and the day was mellow with a golden sun that warmed without overheating. Living in the desert would take a little getting used to for Slade, but he was eager to try. He'd go anywhere to be by Kate's side and he knew she was committed to the Redstone Clan at the moment.

When they arrived at the house, Keith greeted them at the door.

"Right on time." Keith spoke in solemn tones. Slade figured there wouldn't be much joy in this house for some time. The grief was too recent. Too strong.

It would lift in time. The matriarch would not have wanted her family to suffer and eventually they would realize that and be able to come to terms with her loss. It might take years, but healing would come.

Keith ushered them back to the big, family dining room. An informal meal was being laid out on the table and Kate immediately sought the kitchen, helping Valerie and an uncharacteristically quiet Matt Redstone lay out the meal.

Grif entered the room with his little sister and greeted Slade, inviting him to sit while the meal preparations continued around them. Belinda moved listlessly to help with the platters of salad and condiments while the other brothers straggled in, one by one.

"Thank you for coming," Grif began, getting right to business. "I wanted to talk to you about your plans for the immediate future."

Slade nodded. "Kate is my mate. If it's agreeable to you, I would join her here since she is committed to your Clan and I've been roaming for the past few decades. I don't have a permanent home outside my Clan lands and though eventually I'd like for us to move there, as of right now, I think we're needed here."

"More than you know." Grif sighed and Slade could see the weight of responsibility wearing heavy on his shoulders. "I'm going away for a bit. I'm taking Belinda to the forest where she can run free and begin to heal. Being here isn't very good for her right now."

Slade was concerned. For an Alpha cat to leave his Clan to go prowl for a bit wasn't unheard of, but Grif Redstone wasn't just any Alpha cat. He had not only his Clan but an entire army of shifter construction workers and their families that looked to him for leadership.

"Steve and Robert will take over here while we're gone, but they're going to need help. I was hoping you would stay, Slade. Your snowcat will give them hope where little else can right now. My brothers are strong men. Good Alphas. But they are as grief stricken as I am. They'll need guidance I can't give right now. I've heard your people specialize in that." Grif cracked a small, rueful smile as he looked at Slade.

"I'm only half snowcat," Slade was careful to point out. "But I'll do my best to help where I can. My days of prowling alone are over. And I have an ace in the hole." Slade had to smile when he thought of the dynamo that would come at his call. "My great-grandmother will probably come running when she finds out about Kate. She's the real snowcat, with all that implies."

"She's from Tibet?" Grif seemed impressed by the very idea.

"She hasn't been back to the Himalayas since she left to mate my great-grandfather, but yes, she was raised in the mystic tradition and teaches it to every generation of our Clan. She is the most steadying influence I know. Where she travels, peace soon follows. I think she could be of great help here, during this time of upheval."

"Call her," Grif said with great finality. "Today, if possible. I'll call the Lords and make this right with them. I know you run their security when you're not doing special jobs for them. Maybe you could help Steve with that here, if you're so inclined."

"I already talked to Tim and Rafe," Slade admitted. "Just preliminarily. They'd like me to be on-call for special assignments, if needed."

Grif nodded. "That sounds more than reasonable. We'll work out the details, but I'd say all that's left now is to fill in your mate. She's tapping her foot and her arms are crossed," Grif noted, looking pointedly toward the wide entryway to the dining room. "Did you tell her you were moving here yet?"

Kate moved into the room, her expression tight. "No, he hasn't," she said in a very distinct, slightly angry tone. "In fact, we haven't discussed it at all."

Slade turned to her, tugging her down into his lap as he sat at the table. She didn't resist, which was a good sign.

"Kitten, I've seen how committed you are to this Clan and I couldn't ask you to leave them. Especially not right now. I'm way more mobile than you are, with fewer ties to bind me to a particular place. I've been roaming for decades. Let me settle down here with you. It's okay with Grif. All I need now is your agreement and we can begin our life together. What do you say?"

She held out for all of thirty seconds before throwing her arms around his neck and kissing him in front of Grif and all of the Redstone family members who had gathered in the dining room.

"Okay," she whispered against his lips as she drew slowly away.

"Great," Grif broke in. "Then it's settled. Welcome to the Clan, Alpha Snowcat."

Slade cringed a little at the title. Not that he wasn't an Alpha snowcat, but he'd become so used to hiding his dual nature, it seemed odd to have it said out in the open like that. In a Clan like the one Redstone oversaw, with so many different kinds of shifters in it, there were designated Alphas for each species. Since Slade was the only snowcat—and likely would be until he and Kate started their family—he was it. And if they didn't already know after his appearance at the construction site last night, the whole Clan would soon realize there was a rare and mystical snowcat in their midst.

Good thing he was mated to a priestess. When people started showing up looking for spiritual counseling, he could always call on Kate's expertise to help. In fact, he suspected they were going to make a great team.

Everyone took their seats and Slade released Kate so she could sit on the chair by his side. They began eating and conversation turned more general until Grif startled Kate with his next words.

"I spoke with Johan Hager early this morning and extended visitor's rights to him and his immediate family. He tells me that you, Kate, are his long-lost granddaughter."

Kate cleared her throat before answering. "So I was told this morning." She seemed uncomfortable talking about the subject that was so new and unfamiliar to her. Slade took her hand under the table, offering comfort.

Matt laughed from midway down the table, drawing their attention.

"What's so funny, little brother?" Grif asked, seeming intrigued by the youngest brother's reaction.

"I was just thinking of that old children's story. We now have our own real life version of *The Owl and the Pussycat*."

Slade groaned as the others chuckled. It was good to hear laughter—even the subdued kind—in this house that had seen so much tragedy of late.

Later that afternoon when they'd taken their leave of the Redstones and found their way back to Kate's pretty little house, Kate reopened the topic of his move.

"It was kind of you to uproot yourself and move here to be with me, but are you absolutely certain that's what you want? I can just as easily move to be where you are."

"While I appreciate the offer, we both know you're needed here right now and for the foreseeable future. This Clan needs you like no other, Kate. I couldn't ask you to leave them. It wouldn't be fair to you or to them." He kissed her brow, loving the feel of her in his arms. "Besides, I might be able to help too. I have a lot of skills that a Clan this large and diverse can use. And now that I've found you, my roaming days are over. This is as good a place to settle as any. Better than most, in fact. I already like the people and best of all, you're here and you've already decorated a guest room for my great-grandmother." He dodged her hands as she tried to tickle him.

They laughed and he felt the freeing feeling of hope for the future bubbling up from his soul. She was good for him and he swore to the Goddess they both served that he would do all in his power to make Kate's life as fun-filled, happy and loving as he could possibly manage.

"I love you, Kate." He nuzzled her cheek and took her down to the couch in her sparsely decorated living room. There was still a lot to do to make this house a home, but with Kate in it, the hardest part was already solved.

"I love you too," she whispered, and that was the last thing either of them said for quite some time while they christened the comfy new couch in the most delicious way.

# # #

A Word From Bianca D'Arc
About Her Paranormal Series

Since I started writing paranormal romances in 2005, much has happened behind-the-scenes to affect the way in which these stories have been released. Originally, there were two very separate series—the *Brotherhood of Blood* for vampires, and the *Tales of the Were* for werewolves and their werecreature friends.

The main reason for this separation was that each series was with a different publisher. The publisher that originally had my vampire short stories and novellas went out of business some years ago and I began the process of bringing those stories over to Samhain Publishing, which had been publishing my *Tales of the Were* novels. I took the vampire short stories and novellas, expanded them — in some cases significantly —and republished them with Samhain, where they remain as of this writing. Those stories are: **One & Only, Rare Vintage**, and **Phantom Desires**.

I have since added to that series with the novella **Forever Valentine** and the crossover novel, **Sweeter Than Wine**, which is the point where it became quite obvious that all of these stories happened in the same contemporary paranormal world. Matt Redstone plays a significant part in that book.

Those five stories are united by the fact that they follow the love stories of five female college friends. All five find that they are mated to vampires. But there is a sixth college friend and her story is told in the RT Book Award nominated novel, **Wolf Hills**. She is mated to Jason Moore, who is mentioned briefly in the book you have just read. He is the Alpha of a large werewolf Pack in Wyoming, and his brother, Jesse, heads up the Ghost Squad.

At this point, the *Brotherhood of Blood* series will begin to follow that story line, and the next novel in the series, the upcoming, **Wolf Quest**, is Jesse Moore's story. There is quite a bit of crossover now between the *Brotherhood of Blood* and the *Tales of the Were*, but the timing is tricky. The internal chronology of the stories has been, at times, difficult for me to reconcile because of all this confusion in the way the initial stories came out, went out of print, then were re-released.

The *Tales of the Were* series will branch off from this point and follow the five Redstone brothers in a sub-series I'm sub-titling *Redstone Clan*. You'll notice a little graphic to that effect on the next five covers in the series, starting with Griffon Redstone's story, coming later this Spring.

I think I've finally reached the point where the internal chronology will straighten out. The pivotal point for all of these stories seems to have been the Redstone matriarch's death. From here, we'll follow Grif as he takes his little sister out into the wilds to heal, and the mysterious woman he finds fighting her own battles out there.

We'll also catch up with Mag and his vampire friend. And we'll see Steve find the love of his life. As will Bobcat and Matt. With any luck, these stories will come out every few months during the rest of 2013 and into 2014. Where we go from there, I'm not sure yet, but I can guarantee, it'll be a wild ride!

Come over to The D'Arc Side...
WWW.BIANCADARC.COM

One & Only
By Bianca D'Arc

Brotherhood of Blood, Book 1

A deadly crash changes the fate of one lonely vampire.

Vampire enforcer Atticus Maxwell stands at the edge of his own oblivion...until the faint heartbeat of a desperately wounded mortal woman calls him back. The terrible crash that almost took both their lives has brought him a charming, intriguing woman who just might give him a reason to live again.

Lissa was headed for a conference at a resort in a last-ditch attempt to find a job. Instead, on a rain-slick mountain road that almost killed her, she finds the love of her life. A love with the most eligible, reclusive vineyard owner in Napa Valley—one that isn't quite human.

No barrier—not even breaking the news to Lissa's friends—seems too great to hold back their blossoming love. Until they learn the accident that brought them together wasn't an accident at all, but a murder attempt by an unknown enemy.

Atticus saved Lissa once. Can he keep her that way in the face of a renewed threat?

Lords of the Were
By Bianca D'Arc

Tales of the Were, Book 1

An ancient evil is stalking the twin alpha rulers of the werefolk and the half-were woman who is destined to be their mate...if she lives long enough.

Fulfilling her mother's dying wish, Allie climbs a wooded hill just before midnight on Samhain—All Hallow's Eve. At the top, she finds an overgrown, magical stone circle, and her destiny. Waiting for her there are twin alpha werewolves who will be her sworn protectors, her mentors...and the loves of her life. If she lives long enough.

Overprotective is just one word to describe Rafe and Tim. Sexy is most definitely another. But their newfound love and all their skills-both mundane and magical—will be tested by an ancient evil. A hostile human mage and a misguided vampire hunt them, servants to secret plans of the ancient *Venifucus*, a society dedicated to destroying women like Allie.

They will earn unlikely allies, including a half-fey knight imprisoned Underhill for centuries, but will it be enough to battle the evil that stalks them? Will Allie's men be strong enough to let her aid them in her own defense? Only together can were, fey and vampire defeat this latest threat and learn that love does truly conquer all.

Warning: This book contains not one, but two, frisky werewolves intent on capturing their mate in a permanent menage relationship. Rawr!

Keeper of the Flame
By Bianca D'Arc

Dragon Knights, Book 7

A warrior, a maiden...and a passion that could set the whole world aflame.

Despite the fact he is the largest of his half-dragon brothers and better suited to fighting, Hugh has been sent on an undercover mission. Forced to stay in human form, he must discover if the land of Helios is truly the Draconian ally it pretends, or something more sinister.

When he witnesses injustice in the form of a misshapen baby gryphlet kicked out into the cold, he cannot remain in the shadows and watch the child suffer. All he can hope for is that his act of kindness will go unnoticed so his mission can continue.

But someone does notice. When Lera cautiously approaches Hugh, she is drawn to his strange, foreign magic. She is entranced by its irresistible allure -- until assassins come calling and reveal her true identity.

She is Valeria, queen of Helios, Keeper of the Flame. And she has been betrayed. Together they must risk everything to uncover the traitors and reforge the alliance between their lands. Yet beneath their blazing passion, both are still keeping secrets. Secrets that the Sacred Flame will reveal—if their love survives its cleansing fire.

Warning: When a dragon prince and a Flame Keeper come together, the conflagration is definitely too hot to handle!

King of Swords
By Bianca D'Arc

Arcana, Book 1

David is a newly retired special ops soldier, looking to find his way in an unfamiliar civilian world. His first step is to visit an old friend, the owner of a bar called *The Rabbit Hole* on a distant space station. While there, he meets an intriguing woman who holds the keys to his future.

Adele has a special ability, handed down through her family. Adele can sometimes see the future. She doesn't know exactly why she's been drawn to the space station where her aunt deals cards in a bar that caters to station workers and ex-military. She only knows that she needs to be there. When she meets David, sparks of desire fly between them and she begins to suspect that he is part of the reason she traveled halfway across the galaxy.

Pirates gas the inhabitants of the station while Adele and David are safe inside a transport tube and it's up to them to repel the invaders. Passion flares while they wait for the right moment to overcome the alien threat and retake the station. But what good can one retired soldier and a civilian do against a ship full of alien pirates?

And here's a peek at a new book by a friend of mine...

Enforcer's Redemption
By Carrie Ann Ryan

Adam Jamenson has suffered through the worst loss known to man. The only reason he lives day-to-day is to ensure the safety of his Pack. As the Enforcer of the Redwood Pack, it is his job to protect all in his path, though he was unable to protect the ones he held dear. The war with the Centrals is heating up and Adam must try and grit through it in order to survive. Though the broken man inside of him may not want to...

Bay Milton is a werewolf with a past. And a secret. She's met the Redwood's Enforcer only once, but it left a lasting effect. Now she needs to find him or everything he had thought he lost, may be lost again.

Together, they must struggle and find a way to fight their pasts and present in order to protect their future. But the Centrals have a plan that might make their path one of loss and destruction.

For more information visit
WWW.CARRIEANNRYAN.COM

ABOUT THE AUTHOR

Bianca D'Arc has run a laboratory, climbed the corporate ladder in the shark-infested streets of Manhattan, studied and taught martial arts, and earned the right to put a whole bunch of letters after her name, but she's always enjoyed writing more than any of her other pursuits. She grew up and still lives on Long Island, where she keeps busy with an extensive garden, several aquariums full of very demanding fish, and writing her favorite genres of paranormal, fantasy and sci-fi romance.

Bianca loves to hear from readers and can be reached through Facebook, her Yahoo group or through the various links on her website.

Website
WWW.BIANCADARC.COM

CPSIA information can be obtained at www.ICGtesting.com
Printed in the USA
LVOW01s1743110713

342470LV00016B/761/P